The Christmas You Deserve

five festive terror tales

by **Paul Finch**

Top Ten Sunday Times bestselling crime and horror author

Cover art by Neil Williams

https://paulfinch-writer.blogspot.com/

CONTENTS

The Merry Makers – 1

The Unreal – 34

Krampus – 67

The Tenth Lesson – 90

The Stain – 131

THE MERRY MAKERS

I was somewhere in the West Country. That was all I really knew. Part way between Bournemouth and Bristol. I'm aware that sounds vague if not a tad ridiculous. Bournemouth and Bristol are 130 miles apart. I could have been almost anywhere. Or so it felt.

Especially when I had the misfortune to call at Mistletoe Hall.

*

My plan had seemed like a good one initially.

All-day meetings in Bournemouth on December 23, followed by a night in the local Premiere Inn. The following morning, hotfoot it up the M27 and A34 to the M4, and I'd easily make Bristol in time for my afternoon meeting, which, if it ended early, as I was optimistic it would, that day being Christmas Eve, I'd be back on the M4 by teatime, from where it was only

120 miles to London. With luck, I'd be home and celebrating the season by 7pm.

And then it had snowed.

Not heavily. Just enough to put down a light covering on the woods and fields of Hampshire. It shouldn't have been a problem, but of course the UK is a country where autumn leaves stop trains, where, even though we have on-and-off rainfall for much of the year, heavy bursts can still overwhelm our Victorian drainage systems and leave streets flooded. Even then, I didn't anticipate too much trouble. Town centres would be gridlocked as people vacated their offices early in a dash to get home before they were snowed in (by two inches!). But I'd be out in the countryside at that point. I ought to have a clear run. And at first it looked as if I would. Okay, the roads were under snow, but it was paper-thin, so I knew that with a little prudence I could handle it.

Unfortunately, few others adopted the same approach.

Just south of Whitchurch, I found my side of the A34 blocked by a lorry that had skidded and jammed itself crosswise across both carriageways. I doubled back and sought out the A303, only to mire myself in more slow-moving traffic because other inconsiderate drivers had caused similar accidents. By now, of course, my schedule was slipping. But things only went badly awry when I pulled off the main road, seeking passage via the network of narrow country lanes for which this rural corner of England is so famous. My blithe assumption was that at some point soon the sat-nav system would pick me up again and show me another easily navigable route. Stubbornly though, it continued to try to send me back to the A34. I was furious by now. My 1pm meeting had been and gone and all I could do was plough resolutely on in what I felt certain was the right direction, though I had no way to substantiate this (in the age of the sat-nav, so many of us have foolishly discarded our road maps). And now, of course, I was driving recklessly myself, taking turns at random, getting my foot down along straight stretches even though they were mostly single-track lanes.

I saw no other vehicles, no people. I passed lone farmhouses rather than villages, though even these petered out after a while. Those crossroads I came to were either unmarked, or displayed place names I didn't recognise. And all the while, the calm, measured voice of my sat-nav advised that I turn around when possible.

"Bloody thing!" I snapped, wrenching it from my windscreen, only to drop it into the foot-space beneath my feet.

I reached down for it before it got trapped under my pedals, and fleetingly took my eye off the white ribbon of the road. It couldn't have been for more than a second, but when I looked up, that ribbon had curved to the right and suddenly my nearside wheels were thundering through tangles of frozen vegetation. I panicked, fighting the wheel. Snow exploded onto my windscreen as bushes went down under my engine, the left flank of my Hyundai grinding and tearing along the low rock wall, and with an air of grim finality, something *crunching* underneath me.

After I'd come to a stop, I sat numbed, the engine ticking as it cooled.

My windscreen was opaque with snow and shredded greenery. When I turned the key, the only response was a clatter of broken parts. I checked my own extremities to ensure they were intact, and scrambled out, flinching at the biting chill.

Pulling my suit jacket on, I checked the car's front end. There was much damage, none of which I was qualified to diagnose. In addition, my vehicle's front nearside was buried not just in snowy, skeletal undergrowth but in the semi-demolished rock wall, where it looked to have wedged itself in place.

I dug my phone out, though that would be no use unless I knew exactly where I was.

I had no clue what I was going to do next. And when I opted to call Laura, simply to pass on the news, I found that I had no signal. I wasn't as horror-stricken by this as you might expect. Generally, when marooned in a cell-phone black spot, one usually needs to move a short distance to correct it. I donned my fleece and zipped it up, only to wonder if maybe it would be better to wait with the car. It surely couldn't be long before someone else appeared.

But this was not a given.

On all sides, snow-clad meadows rolled to indistinct horizons. There were no roofs; there was no smoke from any chimneys. I didn't even see farm animals. Save for the hiss of the glacial wind, it was completely silent.

More problematic yet, it was turning dark.

My phone told me that it was just after three. Which meant that full nightfall was maybe an hour away at most. Suddenly, waiting didn't seem like an option.

Collecting my overnight bag, I commenced walking. With luck, it wouldn't just help me find a phone signal. Though I had my fleece on, underneath it I wore only a light suit and a thin shirt. The exercise ought to help me keep warm and should not have posed a problem – I was thirty years old and in good health – but my leather, lace-up loafers were hardly ideal. Only two inches of snow carpeted the road, but it seemed softer and more treacherous now that I was treading on it. Several times, I slipped and fell. Meanwhile, the sky darkened, and the temperature tumbled. Shuddering, I checked my phone again and again, but with no luck.

For the first time I began to wonder if this might be *more* than simply inconvenient.

And then I saw a light.

It was a mere pinpoint, far away to my left across open land, its source concealed in the deepening dusk. But it was continuous and bright. I hurried along the road, assuming that at some point there'd be a connecting lane. However, when the light came on level with me, and I still hadn't seen a turn-off, I became worried again. Should I climb the wall and head across country? Not wanting to trespass, I trudged doggedly on. But soon the light was falling behind me. I stopped again, now riven with cold, joints aching, chest wheezing. I checked my phone and was appalled to see that not only was I still minus a signal, the battery was on the verge of expiring.

That decided it.

I clambered over the wall and plodded for several minutes across snow-covered pasture. When I came to a bulwark of darkling trees, I lost the light. Alarmed, I staggered left, and spotted it again, twinkling through leafless, spidery branches. I threaded into a smallish wood. There was less snow in there, though I'd soon reached a narrow road – a driveway, I guessed – which again was covered by an unbroken sheet of white, suggesting that it wasn't used very often. I followed it, anyway, finally entering open space.

Mistletoe Hall stood in front of me.

*

I knew that was its name because there was a tall brick post from which an iron bar protruded. Hung from this bar was an oaken plaque. The words inscribed on it were crabbed and mossy, but I was able to discern them thanks to the light, which shone from a downstairs window where the curtain hadn't been closed properly.

Had I not been so relieved, it might have struck me that the house had seen better days. All I remember on first arriving was that it was an ugly, hulking structure built from dark brick, with shelves of snow on its turrets and roofs. It had many windows, but all save the one I'd seen were heavily draped. None of this mattered as I blundered to its massive front door, hoping against hope that the absence of vehicles and tyre-tracks didn't signify that the occupiers were away. There was no bell, just a heavy knocker, which resounded eerily through a vast, hollow interior.

When there was no response, I struck with the knocker again. More deep reverberations sounded, along with something else: the sudden, muffled thud of an internal door. I hung my head with relief as bolts and chains were withdrawn. The door opened a couple of inches and a white face peered out.

It was a woman of uncertain age, though she was plain-featured and wore her dark hair scraped back and tied into a severe bun. She looked vaguely startled.

"I … I'm sorry," I stammered. "I hope you don't mind …" She tried to close the door, and I thrust my foot into the gap. "Please … I've had an accident. And I'm lost."

She regarded me strangely, as if trying to understand what I was saying.

"Is there any chance I can come in?" The cold gnawed at my very bones.

"For Heaven's sake, Agnes!" came a chiding voice.

Another figure appeared and a hand pushed the door open several more inches. The newcomer was male, and older than the woman by a couple of decades. He was short and tubby, balding on top but with lengthy white hair around the sides, a curled white moustache and white goatee beard.

"What happened to charity and kindness?" he asked gently. The woman stepped aside as he opened the door properly. "Please," he said, "come in."

I tottered inside. "Thanks …"

My first thoughts on entering what appeared to be a kind of lengthy reception passage was that there was no discernible difference in the temperature; my breath still smoked, and the only light, which was a pale yellow colour, was some distance ahead of me. The passage itself was bare; I glimpsed wood-panelled walls, a plaster ceiling, a stone-flagged floor. But I was still grateful to be indoors.

"My name's Tom Kelsey," I said.

My hosts exchanged inscrutable glances, but the man remained affable, shaking hands with me. "James Parnell. This is my sister, Agnes."

The woman regarded me blankly.

"You guys are real life-savers," I said. "But I won't keep you too long. I know you'll be busy on Christmas Eve."

"Oh no … no, no," James Parnell replied. Rather hastily, I thought. "We don't celebrate Christmas here. It's nothing to us."

"If I can just use your phone?" I said. "I'll obviously pay for it. I need to call a pick-up truck or something. Then I need to call my wife …"

My words tailed off because Parnell, rather solemnly, was shaking his head. "I'm afraid we don't have a phone."

"You don't?"

"We lead simple lives out here. We've no call for a phone."

Briefly, and for reasons I couldn't pin down, I felt as if I'd transgressed simply asking for one. "Well, look …" I swung my bag to my hip and unzipped it. "I have my own charger cable. My own phone's dead, but if I could plug it in with this, I'll be able to place a call. I'll pay for any power I use."

He regarded me confusedly, not as if what I'd said had bewildered him, but as though he was trying to come up with an adequate response. Then, abruptly, he smiled. "I'm sure that'll be fine." He offered his palm. "I'll take it to the kitchen."

I handed the device and the cable over. "It won't use much … I promise."

He ambled away. "Agnes, show Mr Kelsey into the parlour. I'll be with you shortly."

I turned to the woman, who, instead of leading me down the passage towards the light, pushed open the door to a side-room. For the first time, she smiled. Rather sweetly – she wasn't as plain as I'd initially thought – but there was a curious degree of firmness there.

The room she showed me into, the so-called parlour, was as bare as the corridor, wood-panelled, with a flagstone floor, a single light bulb overhead, which gave off a dull glow, and heavy, dust-laden curtains on the windows, though one pair were open by a couple of inches, indicating that this was probably the room I'd seen from outside. At least it was warm; there was a small fire burning in the grate, no more than a heap of embers really, but that was adequate because the room wasn't large. There were no furnishings aside from a wooden table in one corner, with two rude benches placed one to either side of it. Before I could pass comment, the door behind me closed.

I turned in surprise, thinking it rather abrupt of her, but then decided that her off-hand manner, along with her lack of speech, might be due to some kind of learning difficulty.

At least, as I say, it was warm. So, I sat down to thankfully thaw out.

And to wait … and wait.

When the door finally opened again, Agnes returned. Previously, she'd been wearing a scruffy old house-robe, as had her brother, but now she'd changed into a floor-length grey skirt, a grey, button-up tunic and a black shawl. To my surprise, she was carrying a tray on which there was food. She set it down, and I saw a bowl of what looked like vegetable broth, two slices of buttered bread, a mug of milk, a folded napkin and a spoon.

I glanced up at her. She nodded, implying that it was for me.

I hadn't eaten all day, plus it would have seemed rude not to. I tucked in, though it was a little disconcerting that my hostess then sat down opposite me, watching closely. As such, I minded my manners, taking only small spoonfuls, dabbing at my mouth with the napkin. Parnell now came in, closing the door and sitting alongside his sister. He too had changed into plain, dark clothes: black trousers, a black tunic, a grey shirt underneath.

"Is the food to your liking?" he asked.

I nodded. "Just what the doctor ordered."

"Excellent. Nothing fancy, of course. Nothing excessive. Just good solid nourishment."

I didn't mention that it could have done with a bit of seasoning, though it wasn't unpleasant even without that.

"When you've eaten," he said, "I'll show you to your room."

"My room?" I lowered my spoon. "I was hoping to make a phone-call."

Parnell frowned. "I understood your phone was not working?"

"Well … if you've plugged it in, it should be recharged soon. Sufficiently for me to make a call, at least."

He considered this. "I'll check in a minute. Fortunately, we always keep a guest room prepared. Even though this is a remote area, you never know who's going to turn up."

"I doubt you'll need to go to that much trouble," I said. "If I can make a call, it's highly likely someone will come and get me."

"Of course. Just so long as you know that if they don't, there is room for you here."

"That's very kind." I continued eating. "Thanks."

They nodded and smiled and continued to watch me, and I felt vaguely irritated that he still wasn't going to check on my phone.

"So …" I ventured, "people *do* come around here occasionally?"

Parnell nodded. “Mainly at this time of year. I think it’s to do with this house. You’ll have noticed the name?”

“Oh, yes, Mistletoe Hall. That’s rather …”

“I expect they think they’ll find feasting here,” he interrupted. “Or some other form of papist idolatry.” He sensed my bewilderment. “You must forgive us, Mr Kelsey. We’re rather set in our ways. Our beliefs do not hold with Christmas as a religious feast. In scripture, no holy days save the Sabbath are recognised, while December 25 as the date of Christ’s birth is completely ahistorical.”

I still didn’t know how to respond. “Each to their own, I suppose.”

“You don’t share these opinions?”

“I’m, erm … I’m irreligious, I’m afraid.” For the first time in my life, I felt awkward admitting this. The twosome watched me, intrigued. “If the signpost’s a problem for you,” I said, looking to change the subject, “why not just take it down?”

Parnell sighed. “Too late. Agnes and I are well known hereabouts as the occupants of Mistletoe Hall. Even if we rename it, it will always be thus. But sometimes it attracts the right kind of people. Your good self, for example.”

He nodded again and smiled. Rather knowingly. Which seemed odd.

“I must confess,” I said, “I didn’t come here because this is Mistletoe Hall.”

“That’s what you may say.” There was a twinkle in his eye.

“It *is* what I say,” I replied.

“So few in that noisy, decadent world are masters of their own fate, wouldn’t you agree?”

I laid my spoon down. "Look, I'm sorry … but, while I appreciate the offer of a bed here, and I certainly appreciate this meal, I'd really like to get home tonight. There isn't somewhere close by where you could drive me, is there? A village where there might be a railway station or a bus stop? Even if it's quite a distance, I'll pay for the petrol."

As before, Parnell gave a sombre shake of his head. "Alas, we have no car."

Immediate other questions piled in the back of my mind.

Surely you travel out occasionally? How do you get your supplies in? What if one of you was taken ill? No phone, no car?

But to voice all this would have seemed unnecessarily impolite. Particularly as I would shortly have my phone back. I finished my food and sat back expectantly.

Parnell sighed. "Well, I hope you don't mind, Mr Kelsey, but Agnes and I retire early."

"Not a problem," I said. "But if I could just have my phone? I'm sure there must be a speck of power in it by now, and I really do need to let people know that I'm safe."

He stood. "I'll bring it for you. In the meantime, Agnes show Mr Kelsey to his room."

They seemed quite adamant that I was to spend the night, which maybe wasn't a bad thing. If the worst came to the worst, and Laura wasn't able to come and get me, at least I had a bed. So, I picked up my bag and allowed the Parnells to lead me out into the corridor, which was now completely dark; whatever faint light I'd seen earlier, it had been switched off.

Parnell melted away into the gloom, and I found myself stumbling in pursuit of Agnes, who walked stiffly and primly, hands folded in front of her. We rounded several corners and mounted a staircase, this too in darkness, turning twice at small switchback landings, though as we arrived on the second one, a light activated overhead. When we reached the top, it showed an upper floor that was also bare of décor. Everything was spotless but the aura was bleak. The glow of a single light bulb dwindled as Agnes led me a merry dance along more corridors. There were so many rooms, all with closed doors, that it was difficult to know how she picked one out for me specifically, but she did, suddenly stopping, opening a door on her right, going inside and flipping a light-switch.

I followed her, entering a room as plain and unadorned as every other part of this place, though it had what looked like a clean bed, a four-poster no less (though minus a canopy), and a single table with a jug and a cup on it. In addition, unlike the landing, it was warm.

"This is great," I said. "But I really don't think I'll need to put you out like this."

She nodded, as if she didn't understand me, or even care to try, and retreated, closing the door. I stood bewildered and not a little bit aggravated. At length, I dumped my bag by the bed and checked out my new surroundings. Beyond the curtain, the window looked down on the forecourt, which thanks to the risen moon, lay frigid under its mantle of white. I discovered that the room was warm thanks to a single radiator pipe passing along the skirting board. The jug, as I'd expected, contained water, which smelled and looked fresh. It was almost as if the Parnells had been expecting me. Or someone. But then I remembered that they claimed to regularly have callers on Christmas Eve.

"Some Christmas Eve." I sat on the bed and rooted in my bag.

There wasn't much in there. Some spare toiletries and the essentials I'd needed for the meeting I hadn't managed to make. There was also a dog-eared paperback. I don't read much, myself, but I'd inherited a box of books from my late father and had grabbed one off the top as I'd left, just in case I'd have some time to kill. As this one was an anthology called *In A Deep, Dark December*, which promised to be *A collection of Christmas hauntings*, it was the last thing I fancied. Frustrated, I stood up. I couldn't understand what was keeping Parnell with my phone. I opened the bedroom door.

She was standing outside.

Agnes.

Facing me from a couple of inches away.

As if she'd been there all the time, staring at the door.

She fixed me with a steady, waxen smile. And made no effort to move out of my way.

"I, erm … I'm sorry," I stuttered. "I was just wondering about my phone."

"There's no power yet," came the voice of James Parnell, standing somewhere out in the corridor. The upstairs light had been turned off, so I couldn't see him. "It's still dead, I'm afraid."

"It's okay …" I was semi-hypnotised by Agnes Parnell's pale, rigid smile. "Perhaps I can get it later?"

"Of course," Parnell said. "Or if not later, tomorrow."

"Tomorrow … yes." And I closed the door again.

The hell with tomorrow! I'd give them an hour, let them get to bed, and then I'd retrieve the phone myself. This whole thing was beyond weird. If there'd been a lock, I'd have turned it. The mere thought of that woman standing sentry outside, gazing blankly at the door, was the most unnerving thing I'd ever known. As it was, though, all I could do was sit on the bed and watch the door from the other side.

As the time rolled by, I became sluggish, torpid. The room was indeed warm, and the stress and anxiety of the day had no doubt taken a toll. I lifted my legs and lay back against the pillow, still watching the door as I counted down the seconds. Another few minutes, I told myself, and I'd go out there and start mooching around.

I've no idea at what point my eyelids began to droop.

*

I snapped awake, and several questions hit me at once.

Firstly, how did I ever fall asleep in this predicament?

Secondly, how long had I actually been asleep?

And thirdly, why was my bedroom in pitch darkness?

I sat up abruptly and went dizzy. Fumbling out, I braced myself on the nearest bedpost. Was it possible that I'd been drugged? My memory of the evening's events was reasonably clear, and I recalled the broth they'd given me. But it seemed like paranoid nonsense – I'd had an exhausting day, after all. But then I wondered again how the bedroom light came to be off; it had been on when I'd settled on this bed. That meant that someone had come in here without my permission.

An even more unpalatable thought struck me. Suppose I wasn't alone in here even now?

I listened. There was no sound … not from anywhere in the house, but that didn't mean a thing. The woman, Agnes, had been right outside my door and I hadn't known about it.

I don't think I'd ever been as disoriented as I was at that moment.

"Is someone here?" I whispered.

Again, no response. Nothing in the slightest.

I was alone surely, but the only way to be certain was to find the light-switch. Not that I could remember precisely where it was. Presumably on the wall near the door, but where was the door? In panic, I jumped to my feet – and went groggy again, swaying where I stood.

A second or so later, I'd recovered enough to scan the blackness, and at last fixed on a square of it that was slightly paler than the rest. I groped my way over there, constantly wondering if I was about to trip over a crouching figure. When I reached the window, I grappled with the dusty curtain, yanking it aside. Below me, the snow-covered forecourt lay sparkling and still. When I turned, the snow-light was sufficient to show me that I was alone. It wouldn't be hard finding the light-switch now. But then I spotted movement down on the forecourt.

It was no more than a fleeting glimpse, but I was suddenly certain that I'd just seen what had looked like an animal disappearing around the side of the building.

I tried to tell myself that I'd been mistaken, but in my mind's eye I could still picture it.

It had been furry and four-legged, and literally in the act of vanishing around a corner. I didn't know what colour it was, I couldn't even be sure what size – somewhere between a large dog and a donkey – but the strangest thing of all was that it hadn't appeared to be walking. I know that sounds ridiculous, but though it had been moving at walking speed, its hindquarters had not been in motion.

It had *glided* out of view.

Letting the curtain fall back, I stumbled to the bed, and sat there, cold.

I quite clearly could not spend the rest of the night here. If nothing else, I had to contact Laura. She'd be out of her mind by now. I crossed my room again, this time on tiptoes, harbouring the unavoidable fear that Agnes Parnell might still be outside my door. When I reached it, I took a few seconds to compose myself before opening again.

Only the empty darkness of the landing greeted me.

The deep silence that seemed to fill this entire house reigned on.

I was half-minded to locate the bedroom light-switch, and give myself something to navigate by, but I resisted. Stealth now felt like the most sensible course. I stole out, heading in the direction where I thought the stairs had been. But before I got to the top of them, I halted, listening. From some indeterminate place, I thought I'd heard a faint metallic squeak, repeated several times in succession – though already it had faded to nothing.

I found the stairs and proceeded down them, stepping lightly. At the lower switchback, I heard that squeaking sound again. Repeating itself over and over, this time coming nearer. I stood rigid, one hand gripping the banister like a claw.

It was so dark down there that I couldn't distinguish the vaguest outline of anything, and yet those squeaks were suddenly so loud that I fancied something was moving just below me. Sweat beaded my face as I waited, the breath tight in my chest. Whatever it was, though, it passed me by, receding again as it headed off to some other part of the house.

Finally, it fell silent.

I had no clue what I'd just heard. But I waited a little longer – several minutes in fact – before continuing down to the ground floor.

Where I went from there was anyone's guess. On first arriving, I'd barely registered the layout of the place. So, I had no option but to explore – and I could only do this by working my way to the nearest wall and groping along it. I've no idea how many doorways I passed or corners I turned. I could only marvel at the size of the building. It was a literal rabbit warren, and still so dark that at no stage could I even see a hand in front of my face.

At which point I heard that metallic squeaking again.

On this occasion it was behind me. *Close* behind me. I didn't wait, but took a passage on the left, walking quickly. And never even saw the door that I strode headlong into. Fortunately, it was ajar, so it swung open easily, though there was still a shuddering impact, and, it might have been my imagination, but I could have sworn that the squeaking sound behind me briefly halted. Before speeding up.

This next room was equally black, but it was warmer than the passageways, and, more perplexing yet, there was a smell of cooking. And I don't mean that plain vegetable broth. I was hit by a glorious array of odours: cooked meats, pastries, all kinds of Christmas spices, nutmeg, cinnamon, ginger. When I collided with the edge of a table, my hands encountered what felt like pies and tarts. I put a fingertip to my mouth, and tasted icing sugar, raisins, jam. Then I struck some kind of candelabra, which duly fell over. I snatched out, just catching it before it hit the floor. In the process, another item was dislodged. This did fall, but it only landed lightly. When I reached down and scrabbled around, I found a box of matches.

Behind me, meanwhile, the door creaked open, and the squeaking thing entered.

I lurched on, meeting a bare brick wall with my hands, which I slid along until I came to another door that was ajar. Assuming it a closet or scullery, I opened it and stepped through – and fell full-length down a steep, stone stairway. The fact it was stone was, on one hand, good: when flesh strikes stone it makes no sound. But on the other, I was viciously pummelled before I reached the bottom.

However, even as I lay down there in a battered heap, my ears were attuned to the room above. Was it my imagination, or did the squeaking sound come to a halt at that upper door? I held my breath, now hearing nothing. Then it occurred to me that whoever or whatever it was needed only to reach for a light-switch, and I'd be lying in full view.

Worm-like, using only my hands, I tried to ease myself away from the foot of the stair. Still, no light came on up there. At length, I'd travelled ten yards or so, following a curving path into what felt like an adjacent chamber. Only there did I stop – and heard a dull *clunk* of woodwork.

Had the upper door just closed?

A muffled squeaking receded across what I assumed was the kitchen.

Even then I waited. What seemed like ages passed before I allowed myself to sit up. I hurt all over, but nothing felt broken. As I got to my feet, my foot touched something that rattled, and I recognised the box of matches.

Desperate for some light, I extracted one match and struck it.

At first, its bright yellow spurt threw a huge area into view. It quickly dwindled, but not before showing me several piles of gaily wrapped Christmas presents. I was so stunned by this that I had to strike another match. Damp brick walls indicated that I was in a cellar area, much of which was indeed occupied by stacks of well-wrapped presents.

And they were all enormous. I swear, any one of them could have contained a bicycle or go-kart or an extra-large doll's house.

But how did this tie in with a family who never celebrated Christmas?

I struck more matches, the fifth and last one guiding me back to the foot of the stair and subsequently throwing light into a deeper, dingier recess, which revealed yet more oversized presents, this batch clearly older as they were layered with dust and cobwebs.

Baffled as well as frightened, I ascended the stair and listened behind the door at the top.

When I pushed it open, the warmth of the kitchen again flooded over me, along with all the aromas of Yuletide. I worked my way around the table to the other door. Stepping out into the passage, I listened again and heard nothing, and reasoning that kitchens were usually at the rear of houses, guessed that I had to be close to a back exit. I went right, moving progressively more quickly as I fancied there was a hint of colder air ahead. Rounding a corner, I saw a smudge of pale grey light. Moonlight reflected from the snow and penetrating a frosted glass panel. But before I was halfway there, that abominable squeaking started up again, now directly in front and coming towards me. I even saw the cause, a dark humped shape rapidly advancing.

I turned and fled, still blind, taking corners at random.

And slammed headlong into another door. This one was firmly closed, and I rebounded from it, my nose stinging, blood on my lips and down the back of my throat.

I coughed and spluttered, the squeaking sound coming up behind me. Almost shrieking, I scrabbled for a handle, found one and depressed it. The door opened and I hurled myself through, banging it closed behind me, bracing my shoulder against the wood. As soon as I'd done this, the blackness in this next room evaporated in a massive glare of light. First it exuded from a fire roaring into existence on a hearth to my right, and then from a succession of candles on all the other sides of me, which also flared to life of their own accord.

I stood blinking.

It wasn't a large room. More a reception chamber of some sort, but compared to the rest of this austere building, it was sumptuously furnished and decked for the season in the most eye-catching manner. My gaze roved bewildered across glistening evergreens, polished woodwork, carved Germanic toys. A Christmas tree stood in a corner, frosted white and hung with scarlet baubles. I even heard carols playing. James Parnell, meanwhile, stood by the crackling fire, in the process of lighting a clay pipe with a lengthy taper.

Gone were his drab, black and grey garments. Instead, he wore green trousers and a green doublet, a golden shirt, crimson stockings, black buckled shoes and ruffled lace at his throat. When he turned to face me, he wore makeup, and not a subtle amount, his features powdered white, his lips deepest ruby, ruby orbs on his cheeks, charcoal streaks where his eyebrows had been.

"Why, Mr Kelsey!" he said, "welcome!" For good measure, he added a hearty "Ho ho ho!"

*

"Holly logs provide the ideal fuel in deepest midwinter, wouldn't you say?" Parnell moved to a sideboard, where an immense silver bowl stood alongside a row of crystal goblets. "Or perhaps you'll warm yourself the more traditional way. Brandy punch?"

I could hardly think straight. "You … you think I'll take a drink from you? After you drugged me earlier?"

"We should have granted you free license? Is that what you're saying? I see you're every bit as entitled as your wretched Roundhead namesake."

"Parnell, what in God's name is going on here?"

He chuckled through his pipe-smoke. "Your sort always calls on the Divine when caught in knavery."

"Knavery?"

"Snooping around our family home. Spying on us."

"I was looking for my phone …"

"Which would have been restored to you on the morrow, had you proved true."

"On the morrow? Had I proved …?" Suddenly, the archaic turn of phrase became intolerable. "*What the hell is this?*"

He spread his arms. "This is what you came to see, is it not? What you always suspected? What your kind always suspect … simply because we live where we do."

"This has to be some kind of game."

"Game?" His laughter faded. He scowled. "What would *you* know about that? Something else our soulless Lord Protector has banned. We have games aplenty, as you can see. And food. And drink. Merry making is our forte. Which of course is what you suspected. Which is why you came here in the first place. An accident indeed."

I turned, unable to take any more of his lunacy, and dashed out into the corridor, now as well-lit as the room behind me. But before I could launch myself along it, something emerged from my right, simply rolled into my path. It was the squeaking thing, the cause of which sound was the four wheels it travelled on.

Had I not already glimpsed it from my bedroom window, I'd have goggled in disbelief.

The only way I could think of it was as a toy horse – set on wheels, as I've said – and yet, while not life-size, much bigger than a normal toy would be, perhaps three and a half feet at the shoulder, with an extra foot added for the wheels, which were rusty and old as if they'd once belonged to a thrown-away pram and now were held in place by leather straps around the fetlocks. It was an odious, moth-eaten thing, purple in colour but patched and darned. It would have looked comical, something from a pantomime, with its floppy, mismatched ears, baubles with beads in them for eyes, and a tail of genuine horsehair, had it not been for the stitched-back lips and the long, yellow, peg-like teeth, which looked distinctly real.

My mouth sagged open as the ghastly beast lifted and flicked its right rear leg, the wheel swinging upright and locking into place, so that it was able to balance on that hoof, which I realised belatedly was a human foot. It then did the same thing on the left, rising up on two legs before turning around to look at me. I don't know what shocked me more: the face of Agnes Parnell, beaming excitedly through an oval hole cut in the creature's throat, or her athletic female form, concealed by her drab, puritanical garb earlier but now outlined snugly in ragged, tight-fitting fur.

"The Hooden Horse," Parnell said, his garish features appearing at my left shoulder.

I jumped away, but in my efforts to also avoid the madwoman in the horse costume, tripped over my own feet and fell onto my backside. Before I could get up again, Parnell was pointing an antique firelock pistol down at my face. With relish, he thumbed back its hefty hammer.

"The Hooden Horse is an import from our home county of Kent, where the custom has sadly died," he explained. "An emotional beast who runs wild with anticipation on the eve of our Saviour's birthday. A beast who must be restrained or havoc will ensue."

As though in full approbation, the horsewoman clashed her front wheels together.

"Parnell!" I shouted. "This is sheer madness …"

"Havoc, Thomas Kelsey! The one thing an arch controller like yourself should fear more than anything else. On your feet, sir."

I had no option. I got up and was marched at gunpoint back into the reception room. But if I'd thought *that* was festively clad, I was in for a shock. There was a door on the other side of it, and when I was pushed through this, I realised that it had only been an antechamber to a much larger compartment.

Amazed, I entered Mistletoe Hall itself.

Clearly, this had once been the beating heart of the gloomy pile that the Parnells had somehow come into possession of. If there'd ever been a medieval structure here, I suspected this was all that remained of it. The walls were stone, but hung with sumptuous, brightly coloured tapestries. The roof, far overhead, was vaulted, supported by great oaken hammer-beams, and now crisscrossed with swags of evergreen. At the far end towered a colossal Christmas tree, perhaps twenty-five feet tall; I imagined that it had been hewn down in some frosty Norwegian forest and brought over here especially. It reached as high as a stained-glass skylight in a slanted section of ceiling, and was hung with ribbons and ornaments, and glowed with myriad electric lights. Down the centre of the room lay a vast banquet table laid with all kinds of festive delicacies. My eyes skated perplexedly over yet more pies, puddings and pastries, over roasted fowl and baked fish, over dates, sweet meats and fat German sausages.

More important than any of this, there were guests. Guests the like of which I had never seen; eight seated one side of the table, eight on the other. Life size effigies, I realised, my blood chilling, lumpen papier-mâché monstrosities clad in gaudy robes. As Parnell prodded me down to the far end of the room, I was able to identify some of them.

Sinterklass in his bishop's garb and mitre, a crozier clamped in his gloved, ring-covered hand. Krampus, with his humped back and shaggy goat's head. Belsnickel, with his bearskin cloak and cap, his Mr Punch features, and his vicious, many-tailed whip.

"As you can see, we're in august company tonight," Parnell said. "Nevertheless, for you we've reserved a place of honour."

A carved wooden throne sat in front of the tree. It was huge and stiff-backed, and engraved all over with images of animals and foliage. But fixed onto each of its armrests there was an open steel clamp.

"Sit!" he commanded.

I did so, and he kicked a lever at the side of the chair, the clamps snapping closed on my wrists. He stepped back, surveying his work. Behind him, his sister rode down the hall on all fours, using her right foot to propel herself, her wheels squeaking.

"The irony," Parnell said. "General Cromwell has provided us with our very own Lord of Misrule."

He placed the pistol on the table, took something else up and, stepping forward, put it on my head. I couldn't see it at the time, but from the feel of it and the jingle of its bells, I gauged that it was a paper coxcomb. It felt like the final indignity, or it might have done, had I not feared that worse was now to follow. How the Parnells thought we could resolve this thing without the pair of them facing time either in prison or a facility for the unhinged, I couldn't imagine. But then, as Parnell commenced some rambling, ludicrous speech about the joy and sanctity of a loyalist Christmas, his sister seated cross-legged, clashing her front wheels together like symbols, his other guests sitting lifeless and twisted, I spotted something to my right that literally set my heart pounding.

It was another of those huge, gaily wrapped packages that I'd seen in the cellar. But this one's lid was open, revealing that it was in fact a sturdy box. Covered in wrapping paper but made from plywood. More to the point, it was empty. Thus far.

I peered at it, sweat-soaked. So distracted that, at first, I didn't realise that Parnell had turned his attention back to me.

"You see how we treat *our* prisoners of note." He was offering me a cup. "We don't behead them. We honour them. Treat them as noble guests, bid them drink and be merry. *This* won't entirely be to your liking, of course, but such is the price of principle, Kelsey. A fine old wassail to us is a heinous offence to a Fifth Monarchist." He chuckled. "We call it *Smoking Pope*."

I gazed at him, uncomprehending.

"Port wine," he explained, "roasted lemons, cloves, brown sugar from the Indies and best Burgundy." A mischievous wink. "And a couple of special ingredients of our own."

Special ingredients of their own.

Close behind him, Agnes Parnell had got to her feet again. She cradled the firelock as she watched with an excitement that verged on the sexual. I glanced at the cup, a large, silver chalice. Whatever brew it contained, it certainly smoked.

More so than any mulled wine I'd ever seen.

Open wide," he coaxed, leaning towards me, a demonic painted puppet. "The wider the mouth, the much better for you."

My wrists were manacled, but my legs were free. So, I kicked out with my left. My foot caught his bulky guts hard, my knee the underside of the wassail cup, which flew from his grasp.

Parnell lurched away, semi-doubled over.

Shrieking, his sister took immediate two-handed aim at me and fired. There were only feet between us, the ancient gun booming and flaring, and just to the side of my head, a heavy ball smashed a fist-sized hole through the throne's backrest. The force of it tipped me over, the backrest splintering, the entire antique structure of the chair coming apart at the joints.

The next thing my hands were free, though I still tumbled backward, head over heels. I got to my feet as quickly as I was able, but my path was already blocked. Parnell had straightened up, while his sister had produced a second firelock.

I turned and ran at the Christmas tree.

It felt like a mad, desperate gamble. The tree was huge, something you'd normally find in a town square. But I'd no clue whether it was sturdy or not, and if I got to the top, there was no guarantee I'd be able to smash my way out through the stained-glass skylight.

I took the chance, anyway, throwing myself up into its lower branches.

As I climbed, it proved a solid structure, but the boughs were flexible and prickly with needles. They jabbed my face and poked my throat. Soon I was smeared with sap, draped in tinsel. Baubles fell and smashed. And then a large one blew apart before I'd even dislodged it. I looked down. Parnell was handing the smoking firelock to his sister, who in her turn, handed him the other.

He took aim again, barrel resting on forearm. And discharged, this second shot demolishing a crystal Nativity.

“Christ's sake, Parnell!” I shouted down. ‘Have you lost your mind!’

He gave a mirthful ‘Ho ho!’, and his sister handed him the first weapon back, now reloaded. I clambered frantically, but still he fired, striking the heel of my left shoe, tearing it away, stinging the whole foot. Up I went, regardless, the tree shuddering, creaking.

A fourth shot zipped through the foliage.

"Damnation!" Parnell shouted, though he didn't sound distressed; more as if he was amused, as if this was all great sport. "So much time since Edgehill, since Marston Moor. My aim has diminished. Ahh … *this* should do the trick!"

I couldn't resist looking back again, just as the horsewoman, her tail twitching as though it actually lived, presented him with a much larger, much heavier weapon.

An honest-to-goodness blunderbuss.

"The Major-General's time is up!" he declared, as he put it to his shoulder.

I hung there helpless, branches sliding through my sweat-moist hands. When he fired, it was a cannon blast, smoke and flame bursting forth. But the recoil tottered him, and because of this his aim was off, nails and screws scything the lower section of the tree, ripping through the foliage, shattering the thick, fibrous trunk.

I clung on all the harder as I tilted forward, the tree slowly keeling. Ornaments rained down; the tearing of green timber filled my ears. When I hit the table, I was thrown the full length of it, scattering food and flaming candlesticks. Only on reaching the end, did the falling tree engulf me, meshing me in more branches, more strands of popping, fizzing lights.

For stunned seconds, I lay tangled in wreckage. It was the cloying reek of gunpowder, making breathing difficult, that dragged me back to wakefulness. Coughing, I fought free of the tree and slid down to my feet. On my right stood a hostess trolley on the top of which sat a richly basted turkey, an ivory-handled carving knife buried to its hilt. Behind that stood the open door. Still dazed, I glanced the other way. Smoke and dust obscured much of the great hall, but I could see enough to deduce that the upper two thirds of the tree had fallen. And with tremendous impact, because the far end of the table, having been struck by a greater spread of branches and heftier weight of trunk, had collapsed.

I pushed the trolley out of my way. Waiting, listening. Hearing only the distant strains of the carol concert. Still nothing moved, which made the motionless papier-mâché figures even eerier. The four closest to me had survived and continued to regard each other across the table.

Until the closest one, Belsnickel, twisted in his seat. Rose up. And faced me.

I stood nose-to-nose with a leering, garish horror that perfectly matched the Tyrolean nightmare from which it had been conjured.

All I could do was scream.

And more by instinct than design, reach out, snatch the ivory-hilted knife, and swing it.

Belsnickel's head came off with a single blow. But the crudely made torso stayed upright and lurched towards me. I hacked and slashed, paper and cotton wool guts spilling out.

As quickly as it had come to life, it died again.

And was cast aside, a primitive, broken toy.

Agnes Parnell, the horsewoman of Mistletoe Hall, rose up from behind it. She had survived the fallen tree, and advanced on me underneath the table. I threatened her with the blade as I retreated. She watched me levelly, her waxen features dotted with sweat, her teeth set in a grimace that was easily as fiendish as that of the Hooden Horse itself. I spun out into the antechamber, halting only to grab the bowl of brandy punch and hurl it at the blazing hearth. Flames ballooned, igniting the stockings dangling from the mantel, roaring up the swags of evergreen, travelling at speed across the rich pile rug, the smaller Christmas tree erupting in a blinding sheet of flame.

The horsewoman had now come to the door, but a fiery barrier lay between us.

Taking my chance, I fled again.

The whole house was now illuminated, a sure sign that Parnell had thrown some kind of central switch to bring his maniacal Christmas party to life in one swoop. The austere part of it was lit by dim, brownish bulbs, but I needed to turn only a couple of corners before finding the passage to the front door. When I reached it, inevitably, it wasn't just bolted but locked. And with no key sight.

Then I heard it again, that damnable squeaking.

Blundering left into the room they'd called the parlour, I lugged the curtains aside, finding sash-windows, but on fitting my fingers underneath the closest, could only lift it a couple of inches. The same applied to the next one, and now I could hear those wheels in the corridor outside. I tried to lift the nearest bench but found that it had been screwed to the floorboards.

The door to the parlour crashed open. Bright light, intense heat and a foul stink poured in.

I ran at the window myself, using the bench as a springboard, arms around my head. The glass exploded outward, the impact all but knocking me senseless. I landed on hard, snowy ground, jangling shards falling around me. Streaming blood, weakened by shock, I stumbled across the forecourt, vaguely aware that the room behind me was filled with smoke and fire.

My heart hammered as I plunged into the trees. I was whipped and torn by branches, and certain that all the way an immense fireball followed me, igniting everything it touched, its hellish, blazing wheels squeaking … squeaking …

I lost all sense of direction and when I fought my way to the drive, took a gamble that heading left would not lead me back to the house. My luck held, better than I could have hoped. When I reached the road, the snow still lay firm and crisp, untrammelled by tyres. Nothing had been along here for hours. But now a horn howled, and a pair of headlights dazzled my world. The HGV slid thirty yards before its brakes locked, hitting a standstill only inches short of me.

Gasping, I worked my way around to the passenger door and clambered up.

"Lord almighty!" came the voice inside.

I threw a glance behind, and through leafless trees, saw flames rising ferociously, turning the whole of that sacred night a livid molten red.

*

Laura and I are no longer together.

It's not just that I don't do Christmas anymore. Laura was always a caring girl, and if that was all it was, I feel sure she'd have come to tolerate it. She'd have coped with the fear factor too, though that would have challenged her more. I admit that I don't travel much these days, especially when the end of the year approaches and the nights fall early and the leaves turn crisp with frost, but there is rhyme and reason to this.

It's an overused phrase, 'burned to the ground', but that's what Mistletoe Hall did. Thanks to the DIY gaslines that fed its many fireplaces and even some of its candles, an astounding conflagration left only a blackened heap of ash and char.

And bones, of course. The older bones in boxes, and the newer bones – which, as it happened, came from only *one* person.

Perhaps you'll understand therefore, why any sound that could now be construed as metallic squeaking unnerves me. Or why the faintest scent of burn – bacon too long in the pan, or the pungent aroma when a candle is snuffed out – has me looking behind doors, scanning every street and passage.

Even so, as I say, Laura could have dealt with that; I feel certain.

What ultimately did for us was the suspicion. Even now people whisper and cast me strange glances. And why not? It wasn't just that when I emerged from that raging crematorium, I was battered, bruised and bleeding as if I'd been in a hard fight. Or that later on, the story I'd told and the insanity I'd described seemed too preposterous to be true. It wasn't even that I'd shrieked hysterically at my lorry-driving rescuer to get us away, and that when he grabbed his phone to contact the emergency services, I tried to wrench it off him and shrieked into his face again. It was more the words I used.

'Let them burn ... let them burn! Good God man ... all heretics should burn!'

THE UNREAL

Hetherington had been told to approach the building through its side-gate and knock on the fire-exit door behind the row of dustbins. He did so, and waited, breath pluming in the frozen evening air. No lights showed on this side, but that was probably because there were no windows. The Ambridge Theatre towered above him, an edifice of grimy, Victorian-age brick. But he'd been assured that if he was here for seven pm, someone would eventually admit him. As the wait dragged on, Hetherington shivering in the snow-filled yard, a muffled clamour of revelry drifted from the direction of the town centre, the product of loutish gangs stumbling drunkenly from one glitzy, Christmas-bedecked bar to the next.

There was a *clunk* on the other side of the door, and it cracked open, warm light spilling out. "Alan Hetherington?" a voice with a soft northern accent enquired.

Hetherington nodded.

The man standing there was somewhere in his mid-sixties and rather paunchy. He wore a flowery shirt and bowtie, and a sheepskin coat. His thinning white hair was scraped back and tied at his nape in a small ponytail. He offered a plump, pink hand.

"Ted Lampwick … Theatre Secretary."

Hetherington shook it and entered, finding himself in the theatre's lobby. It was opulent in the traditional style, bright light from a large chandelier embossing gilt paintwork and crimson brocade. On his immediate right, a staircase led up into gloom. Beyond that, a pair of double-doors stood closed, though a brass plaque above them illustrated the seating arrangements in the auditorium. On the other side of that there was a service counter, its queuing area marked out by brass poles and red velvet ropes. Overhead, ropes of glistening evergreen hung in loops along the curtain rails. In the farthest corner, a tall, frost-white Christmas tree towered halfway to the ceiling, dangling with gold and scarlet baubles. Clusters of tinsel glimmered from behind the framed black-and-white stills adorning the walls, each one depicting a past production. Ted Lampwick, in varying stages of youth and middle age, featured in several of them.

Lampwick closed the fire-exit door, but only after glancing curiously around outside. "Alone, are you?" he asked, sounding surprised.

"That's how I normally do it," Hetherington replied.

"Seriously?"

Hetherington was amused by his host's startled tone.

"Pays dividends, trust me. Surely, you've watched some of these TV ghost-hunting shows, where there're umpteen people running around the building? The viewers are focused on the main presenter, so they never know where any of the others are. They hear knocks, bumps, the creaking of overhead floorboards, and are seriously asked to believe it's spirit activity when the reality is it could be anyone. None of that for me and my internet audience. When I do these, I fly solo. I hold my vigils alone in otherwise empty buildings. If I *do* hear something, I can investigate in the full knowledge I'm the only living presence there."

Lampwick didn't look any less unnerved by that. "Well … you're braver than me."

"It's not about being brave, Mr Lampwick, it's about being rational. You'd be amazed at some of the simple explanations I've found for so-called ghosts. Wind in faulty chimneys, joists expanding through temperature change …"

"And you're happy to spend Christmas Eve doing *that*?"

Hetherington smiled as he pulled his gloves off and tucked them inside his parka. "I'm an atheist, Mr Lampwick. I don't believe in God. Therefore, I don't believe in Christmas. Is that wrong of me?"

Lampwick shrugged, leading him across the lobby to the double-doors. En route they passed a poster-board bearing images of the theatre's last production, which apparently had been some kind of larger-than-life puppet show:

A Christmas Carol

Beneath the ornate heading, a piece of extravagant artwork depicted Scrooge cowering before a meagre fire in a grate, while the huge, shadowy form of the Spirit of Christmas Yet-To-Come, garbed all in black, with scythe in hand, lowered over him. Beneath that there were stills from the actual production, life-size marionettes interacting with real actors. Hetherington had heard about this beforehand; ingenious no doubt, but it all sounded very art-house, and of course there was that irritating Christmas aspect.

"It seems to me that doing this tonight of all nights you're depriving yourself a bit," Lampwick said, opening the double-doors. "Don't you have a party to go to?"

"Why celebrate something I don't believe in?"

"You don't have a family?"

"I have a family, but no-one in our house believes in God."

Lampwick regarded him coolly, perhaps wondering if this was a true description of life in the Hetherington household or a stipulation for it.

Hetherington returned the gaze blankly.

He was a tall man, spare of physique, with a mop of copper-red hair and pale features seemingly much younger than his forty-four years. It was a gawky, boyish look, which Hetherington didn't care for much, but he always made up for it with his direct manner and forthright views. Not that he saw any point in antagonising people needlessly. He didn't bother adding that his feelings went much further than he'd admitted to; it *empowered* him, not celebrating Christmas. To most people the once-holy feast was nothing more now than a piss-up anyway, but they still embraced it with ludicrous, ritualistic motions, not to mention indulging in lavish spending they could ill afford. None of that for him. He wasn't dancing to anyone's tune, especially not some big, imaginary sky-fairy.

Beyond the double-doors, Lampwick led him down the auditorium's left-hand aisle. This room might be the heart of the theatre, but it wasn't enormous, with sufficient seating perhaps for one hundred and fifty people and maybe eighty more on the balcony upstairs. The closest Hetherington normally got to theatres was seeing them on TV talent shows, so he'd been expecting something much more spacious, perhaps with elaborate cornicing along the edges of its vast ceiling, and another chandelier, a truly colossal thing, suspended in the middle. But in fact, the "house lights", as Lampwick referred to them, were shaded bulbs located at regular intervals on the auditorium walls, while the stage was only raised four feet from the floor and no more than thirty yards across from one wing to the other. At present, the curtain was drawn back, and the stage was bare except for a single solitary figure standing just to the right, its head drooped. Hetherington made a doubletake before he realised that this was one of the marionettes. By the looks of its threadbare dressing-gown and nightshirt, and the lank white hair protruding from under its nightcap, this was Scrooge.

It was an ugly thing, hanging there stiff and motionless, the barely visible wires trailing up to some dim, indefinable place high above the stage. But it was comical too in a juvenile kind of way. Why go to all this trouble, and it must have been a lot of trouble, to have puppets interacting with real actors? Why not just use a fully live cast? Hetherington supposed it wove a kind of magical festive aura for the little ones, but for any adults unfortunate enough to get roped into sitting here, it must have been a yawn.

A bit like the entire money-spinning con that is Christmas itself ...

Behind the marionette, meanwhile, the stage's rear wall was masked by painted scenery representing a

London skyline from long ago: rookeries, chimney pots and the unmistakable dome of St. Paul's cathedral.

"*A Christmas Carol*," Lampwick explained somewhat unnecessarily. They halted midway down the aisle to appraise the stage. "A festive special, I suppose you'd call it. Not part of our normal roster. A travelling roadshow put it on. We'll be striking this set on Boxing Day and starting work on the Panto. That opens in mid-January. We're doing *Rumplestiltskin*. Should be fun … it's our own version of course, full of ghosts as well as the main goblin."

"Spooks seem to be a running theme in this place," Hetherington said, unable to keep a hint of disdain from his voice.

Lampwick glanced sidelong at him. "Presumably they are for you too?"

"Disproving their existence is my thing."

"Even so, for someone who definitely doesn't believe in the afterlife … to spend all your time holding ghost-watch vigils …?"

"There's no contradiction there," Hetherington said. "My investigations are based entirely on science."

"Ah yes … wind in chimneys and such."

"If the unexpected occurs and I do uncover something bearing further examination, I confidently expect it to fall well within the laws of physics."

Lampwick pondered that, shrugged, and then crossed the front of the stage and took a stairway down, providing further commentary as he did, explaining that he wanted to show Hetherington the entire place before leaving him here alone.

They descended the stair to a small anteroom with doors leading left, right and straight ahead. Go right, according to Lampwick, and you entered the backstage area. Straight ahead was the coffee bar, and left was the entrance to the main theatre bar. Lampwick headed backstage first. This was a cramped rabbit warren of twisting passages and tiny, damp-smelling rooms: changing rooms for the most part, but also props and costume storage, and then the Green Room, which was a much larger area lying directly beneath the stage.

The Green Room was littered with the detritus of the recent production: top hats on tables, a row of wall-pegs hung with shawls and double-caped greatcoats, bags of fluffy white polystyrene balls that had been used as fake snow, a crutch without an owner – and the Marley's Ghost marionette. This latter was slumped on a bench at the far end of the room, a smallish, grey-faced figure clad in once dandified but now shabby Regency-era clothing. The left shoulder of its frockcoat was noticeably frayed and torn, which may or may not have been deliberate, but it added to the effect, as did the gleaming chain with which its upper torso was wrapped, and the dirty bandage bound around its head as though in support of its lower jaw. In the middle of its bald scalp and the backs of its hands, there were tiny metal hooks through which the puppeteers' wires would be threaded.

Just to satisfy his curiosity, Hetherington approached the slouched figure, reached down and rapped on the back of its head. It was made of wood and sounded hollow.

"Creepy things, if you ask me," Lampwick said.

Hetherington adjusted his pack, which was now getting heavy on his back, its straps digging into his shoulders. "People often say that about dummies and effigies. The answer lies in our subconscious. Some deep instinct says 'these things look like us, but they actually aren't us … so it's a kind of camouflage, and that has to be bad'. You see, it's all about understanding the science."

"If you say so." Lampwick continued with the tour, showing Hetherington up a shorter flight of narrow steps to a single door. "This was once the rear stage-door," he said. "But we built an extension on the other side." And indeed, beyond that there was a more modern area, a black steel stairway leading up to what apparently were new rehearsal rooms and, directly ahead, a straight corridor with a tiled floor diminishing into complete darkness. "It looks menacing, but there's another fire-exit down there," Lampwick added. "Takes you straight out onto the road at the back."

"Good," Hetherington replied. "I parked my Subaru out back. Will it be okay overnight?"

Lampwick looked uncertain. "I suppose so … it's cold, snowy. Can't think there'll be too many bad 'uns about."

Hetherington wasn't totally encouraged by that, but he had no choice in the matter. His hotel was a good twenty-minute drive away, which would be a fifty-minute walk carrying a heavy backpack, while taxis were prohibitively expensive on Christmas Eve and notoriously unavailable. He followed Lampwick back through the backstage area to the anteroom, and down into the theatre's basement bar. This was a large, open-plan chamber. It possessed a faint smell of sour beer, but everything else was in good order; it was neatly carpeted, with leather seating and polished pub tables and yet more theatrical photographs cladding the tastefully papered walls. The bar-top had been polished until it shone, rows of optics glinting in the shadows behind it.

"As we agreed before, the bar itself will need to stay locked," Lampwick said, as they walked past it to a narrow passage on the left, where there was another fire-door and a wall-to-ceiling cupboard fastened with a shiny padlock. "We're not making assumptions about your character, Mr Hetherington, but it would be more than the Bar Manager's job is worth to allow someone he didn't know uncontrolled access to that area."

"I understand." Hetherington waited while Lampwick produced a key and unlocked the cupboard. An array of junction boxes and electrical cables was revealed.

Lampwick glanced around. He seemed less nervous than earlier, but in the dimness of the bar's low-key lighting, his eyes were limpid and grey. "I understand you requested the power be turned off?"

"That's correct."

"You're absolutely sure about that? It'll turn the central heating off too."

"I'm well wrapped, so I'll happily sacrifice the warmth to get rid of the light. I don't want any lights at all, not even the emergency lights."

"Well …" Lampwick indicated a row of breaker switches. "This is how you do it. It'll be very dark, though. The whole purpose of theatres is to insulate their audiences against the world of the real."

"I want *complete* darkness," Hetherington confirmed.

"You'll get that down here especially – almost no natural light penetrates to the basement area. But …" Briefly, Lampwick looked amused. "Is it really necessary? I mean, do ghosts need it to be dark in order to come out? And if there's no such thing as ghosts, why bother turning *any* lights off?"

"It doesn't matter to me personally whether it's dark or light," Hetherington replied, mildly irked by the question. "But my internet show has a big audience, and they have expectations."

"Ah … yes, so it's about entertainment as well as science."

"Something has to pay the bills."

"Yes, of course. Well …" Lampwick sighed, as if he'd tried to warn the visitor against this folly, "… turn this lot off, and you'll have what you want. It will also de-activate the alarm, which won't matter so much while you're in here of course, but the security cameras will be turned off too."

"That's okay. I have my own cameras." Hetherington tapped his backpack. "Any footage I shoot needs to be copyrighted to me anyway, so it's best if no-one else films."

That's bollocks of course, Lampwick, Hetherington thought to himself, *but the truth is I don't want someone else making copies of this event, and then doctoring their own videos to show things that never happened.*

"As you like …" Lampwick clapped his hands together. "Okay, I'll leave you to it."

Hetherington followed him through a lower section of bar, and up a different stairway from earlier, an even steeper, narrower one, which connected directly with the theatre lobby. Here, the Secretary halted to pull on a pair of suede driving gloves.

"I wonder," he said. "Was it worth it?"

"Worth what?" Hetherington asked.

"I can see you're a principled man, Mr Hetherington. But are those principles worth what happened to Roger Shelburn?"

Ahhh … here we go.

"Roger Shelburn took his own life," Hetherington said.

Suddenly Lampwick was being very meticulous about donning and adjusting his gloves. He pointedly wouldn't meet Hetherington's gaze. "Surely that was because his career had been ruined?"

"His career as a fraud, you mean?"

"I've often wondered … is it *really* fraud? You tell people their deceased loved ones are happy in the afterlife, and those people go away reassured. Does it really matter if you don't have a clue whether the afterlife exists or not? You still make people happy."

"Once or twice it's probably no big deal. But Roger Shelburn made a career out of it. He had his own TV show."

"So?"

Hetherington had to suppress a snort at such gullibility. "But if it's all untrue ...?"

"Again, does it matter if it makes bereaved people more content?"

"Shelburn was a charlatan," Hetherington declared. "That's all I'll say on the matter."

And you, Mr Ted Lampwick, can like it or lump it.

"Well, I don't have particular views on this, if I'm honest," Lampwick said, almost as though he'd read Hetherington's mind. "I have to say, I've never really thought the Ambridge haunted myself, and I've been a member over forty years. There are no specific stories; it's just an eerie old building, I guess. If there's any spirit here at present …" he glanced at the lobby's festive brocade, "I'd say it was the spirit of the season. Not that this is always a good thing."

"It isn't?" Hetherington was puzzled by that.

"Well, they say Christmas is what you make it … that you get the Christmas you deserve, and all that."

"Good job I don't do Christmas."

Lampwick headed to the fire-door, muttering something in response that sounded like "Let's hope it doesn't do you."

"I'm sorry?" Hetherington asked. "Missed that."

Lampwick opened the door, and a waft of icy air blew in. "I said good luck to you."

"Okay … thanks."

"One last thing," Lampwick said. "When are you planning on leaving tomorrow?"

"First light … half past eight, nine-ish."

"If you throw the breakers back on first, and whichever door you leave through, make sure you close it after you. I'll be popping in mid-morning on my way to my daughter's for Christmas lunch, to check everything's okay. And *I'll* put the alarms back on." Lampwick halted in the doorway. "You're absolutely sure you want to do this?"

Here we go again.

"I'm sure. And thanks for your concern, but I've done it many times before."

"Not *here*."

"No, not here," Hetherington agreed. "But then *you* don't believe this place is haunted either."

"No, but then I've never stayed here overnight, not on my own."

In the dark, when there's nobody else here ... eh, Mr Lampwick?

Lampwick smiled, again as if he'd just read Hetherington's inner thoughts. Then he departed into the blackness and the snow, shutting the fire-exit door behind him.

"Cute," Hetherington said aloud, walking back across the lobby. "A last-ditch attempt to unsettle me. Gotta give you credit, Lampwick. Once an actor, and all that …"

*

Hetherington emptied his backpack and unfolded his tripods and spent the next half hour deploying his devices: his heat monitors, his motion-sensitive cameras, his audio recording instruments, all the usual kit that no self-respecting ghost hunter could be without. When every part of the building was covered, he headed back down into the lower bar area, glancing at his watch. It was just on nine.

Excellent. Always start at nine if you can.

He hit the row of breaker switches, plunging himself into ultimate darkness.

Almost no natural light penetrates to the basement area ...

"Not a problem." Hetherington switched on his night-vision goggles, bringing everything into fuzzy green relief, and activated his goggles-cam and mic. He made his formal introduction to the subscription-paying audience who at some point soon – preferably before New Year – would be tuning in to *Fear Itself*, his regular internet show, and walked back upstairs to the auditorium and down its left-hand aisle.

"So here we are," he said, clambering up onto the stage while addressing his as-yet non-existent viewers. "This is going to be a long, lonely Christmas Eve, but hey ... these are the sacrifices I make for you guys."

To stage-right, access to the wings was gained by a curved brick archway, a huge chunk of authentic

Victoriana. This was an actual part of the theatre's fabric, and no doubt had been worked into the sets for many plays in the past. It would be particularly useful for *A Christmas Carol*, he supposed. More useful to Hetherington, though, was the chair he'd seen sitting in the back of it. He brought the chair out and positioned it in the very middle of the stage, facing the auditorium. This was where he intended to keep his vigil, with occasional patrols around the rest of the building to break the monotony (it was a good thing his shows never went out live – they'd prove a big switch-off if they did).

Before sitting and making himself comfortable, Hetherington scrutinised the life-size Scrooge puppet standing up close. Less detail was visible in the night-vision's green mist. With head drooped, its face was completely indistinguishable aside from its long, tapering nose. In terms of shape, the figure was bone-thin – almost emaciated, like a suspended corpse. The fact it would be hanging just behind and to his left was added unpleasantness.

Determined to push such nonsense from his mind, he shoved his chair backward a few feet, so that at least it hung in his eye-line. Then he settled down.

The chair, which was hard and stiff-backed, was uncomfortable, but that was good – the last thing he wanted was to drop off to sleep. Murmuring these thoughts to his viewers, he appraised the auditorium as it stood empty in front of him. Night-vision wasn't perfect; but at least he could distinguish its basic dimensions; the rows of seating, and the two downstairs aisles. It was only when he glanced up to the balcony that he glimpsed what he thought was a person.

Hetherington blinked once, twice – then stood up and walked to the front of the stage.

He had to be mistaken. Perhaps the fogginess of his vision was playing tricks on him? But it definitely looked as if someone was sitting in one of the seats up there. In the extreme right-hand block, three rows up from the front barrier.

"Hello?" he called hesitantly. "Mr Lampwick?"

But it surely couldn't be Lampwick. He'd left, and the whole place was locked up. And there was nobody else here, or there wasn't supposed to be. The shape on the balcony didn't respond, or even move, but the more Hetherington stared up at it, the more it resembled a seated figure, possibly wearing a heavy overcoat.

"Hello!" he shouted again, more belligerently, his voice echoing to the high ceiling.

Still the figure sat motionless.

"Okay," Hetherington said under his breath, jumping down from the stage.

Every challenge has to be met. That's the way of it on Fear Itself.

He walked briskly up the left-hand aisle, passed through the double-doors into the lobby, and turned at the upward staircase. When he got to the top, he halted. There was an open space on this first level, with comfortable armchairs and sofas, probably for audience members to enjoy coffee during intervals in performances. There were also two brass-handled single doors, one on the left and one on the right. No doubt these corresponded with the two aisles leading down through the balcony seating. From below the figure had been on the right, so it would now be on the left. Hetherington went straight to that door, only to realise that his brow was greased with sweat – which surprised him. He'd been in similar situations before, but something about this one felt slightly different, and he didn't know why.

Odd how that figure didn't move at all. Not so much as an inch.

One thing was sure, he couldn't afford to falter. His goggles-cam always provided the best footage. It enabled his audience to see exactly what he saw. They'd tolerate some degree of editing of course, but if there was a break in the action now, when they'd expect him to go bravely through this door and confront his fear, it wouldn't look good.

He swung the door wide and tramped boldly down the stepped aisle, already able to see the seated shape from behind: it had broad shoulders, and a mass of unruly hair, on top of which an immense rather ridiculous looking hat was perched. It was only when Hetherington got alongside it that he realised his mistake.

No hat, but a holly wreath; no overcoat but a set of fur-trimmed winter robes.

Not the delicate, vaguely camp Ted Lampwick, but the big, robust frame of the Ghost of Christmas Present.

By its obvious wig and fake beard, and its garish face-paint, not to mention its slack-angled head and the flat wooden hand on the armrest next to it, in the middle of which another tiny metal hook was visible, it was obviously one of the marionettes. But just to be sure – because his audience would expect that – Hetherington sidled along the row. Once in reach of the figure, he toed at it warily, and pushed it. It was solid, but jointed and light, probably balsa wood under all that festive regalia. It slumped sideways.

"Someone had nothing better to do today, putting that thing up here," Hetherington intoned, edging back to the aisle. "Possibly our friend, Mr Lampwick, Theatre Secretary. I suspect he thought he saw us coming." Hetherington always referred to himself in the plural during his show commentaries, as though whatever he did or said, his viewers would unquestionably be on his side. Before leaving, he glanced back down at the stage; he could make out his chair and the Scrooge figure. Everything was as he'd left it, except …

He advanced down the aisle to the railing.

Had the Scrooge figure turned slightly?

It was difficult to be sure from this distance, but it now seemed to be facing the chair rather than standing side-on to it.

It was suspended of course, so the air currents Hetherington had caused when leaving the stage might have accounted for that. It barely felt worth bringing it to the attention of his viewers, but Hetherington did so anyway as he re-ascended the aisle, pushing out onto the first level and descending the stair to the lobby.

The next problem came when he reached the double-doors to the auditorium.

They were closed, as he'd expected; apparently, they were on swing-hinges to ensure they couldn't be left open during performances. But when he pulled them, they wouldn't budge. Thinking he was supposed to push, he tried that – but there was no give.

"What the hell …?" He pulled again, hard, yanking at the handles, putting his back into it. This time the doors moved slightly, which indicated they hadn't accidentally locked themselves when he'd gone through them before. Instead, it felt as if … it seemed ridiculous, but it felt as if someone was holding them on the other side.

"This is beyond a joke, okay!" he shouted through the gap. "I mean the puppet upstairs is one thing, but this is infringing on the terms of the contract I signed with your Chairman. I was supposed to have full access to all areas except the bar and the office. I should also remind you I've got cameras everywhere. You and your mates will look a bit foolish capering around in the dark like schoolkids."

There was no sound from the other side, not a hint of movement. Hetherington tugged at the two handles again, to no avail.

"Sod this!" he said under his breath.

He took the downward stair connecting with the basement bar, crossing its lower area first, seeing and hearing nothing untoward. But in the upper bar, he halted in his tracks.

In its furthest recess, another figure was seated.

At one of the bar tables.

Dressed all in white.

Fresh sweat prickled Hetherington's brow.

After calling out, and the figure remaining motionless, he ventured forward. It seemed a safe bet that this was another of the marionettes. The Ghost of Christmas Past perhaps.

When he got close, it was decked in a white silk gown, a white silk cape with a peaked hood, and an oval white mask that was featureless except for symmetrical holes cut for the eyes. Only when he pushed at it did it shift position, *clacking* as its wooden parts jostled together. As he'd suspected, and hardly a problem – except that it hadn't been here when he'd come through earlier. Okay, Hetherington couldn't swear to that, but surely when all the lights had been switched on, he'd have noticed it?

"I'm now even more suspicious that someone is playing games here," he said, backing away. "If not, I apologise to the Ambridge Theatre membership. If they are, however … well, we might play some games of our own before the end of tonight."

So thinking, he entered the anteroom, but instead of going back up to the auditorium, took the door to the backstage area. He moved from one narrow section to the next, always aware of the deep darkness filling the spaces behind him. He couldn't help admitting that if there was someone here, they were doing a damn good job of lying low. In the Green Room, Marley's Ghost was seated on the bench, as before, head bowed. Everything else appeared normal too.

Hetherington re-ascended to the stage by its steep back-stair, sidled around the scenery and slumped into his chair. As an afterthought, he glanced at the figure of Scrooge. It was indeed turned in his direction, as he'd seen from the balcony. In addition, it seemed a little closer than it had been previously. When he'd first arrived here, he'd placed his chair about six or seven feet away from the hanging shape. Now it looked more like four or five. But again, maybe this was due to a disturbance in the air. He glanced overhead. Even with night-vision goggles, nothing was visible up there, just an indistinguishable mass of wood, metalwork and cables, a gantry no doubt for the puppeteers, plus runners, wheels, pulleys. All movements of hanging puppets were explainable. But he couldn't help wondering if Lampwick might be lurking up there too. Well, let him; the static cams would catch him at some point. There was one thing Hetherington would take great pleasure in. In the morning he'd inform Lampwick exactly why he'd come here; not because the Ambridge Theatre was a famous hotspot on the paranormal investigation trail, not because it was famous for anything in fact, at least nowhere outside this unimportant little post-industrial dump of a Lancashire town. But because he'd been dared to.

He deactivated the goggles-cam, before filching the phone from his pocket and running back through his messages. He found the relevant one straight away, and cheerfully played it back to himself.

"You know … Mr Hetherington," a harsh female voice said, quaking with anger. "All my Roger ever did was offer people hope in a difficult world."

She was another one of course, he thought scornfully. Stella Shelburn, or Stella Mordrake to use her professional name. She was a stage witch or magician, or some such nonsense. Maybe *her* act was now in trouble as well; guilt by association and all that. Hetherington hoped so.

"I'm not denying that Roger made money out of his medium tours," the enraged voice added. "Of course he did … he was a showman. That was his career. But no-one forced those people to attend, no-one tore the cash out of their pockets. You didn't need to run that big exposure on him on your website …"

It was a miracle no one had exposed the conman before, Hetherington reflected. *It hadn't been difficult to catch him. A few plants in the audience to make it look as if the spirits really were telling him personal secrets – easy enough to identify those goons. A not especially advanced hologram show, to create the illusion that spirits were trying to materialise ...*

"If you're so hot on disproving the existence of the other realm, you ought to take a real plunge, Hetherington! Don't be going to old castles that have now become visitor centres, where you've got all the mod cons you need. Or stately homes where there's always an attendant in case you run into trouble. Try a real leap in the dark, Mr Alan bloody Hetherington! Try the little-known Ambridge Theatre …"

Hetherington snapped the phone off.

"And yadda yadda," he said. "Well, here we are, Ms Mordrake. Not only in the theatre, but on the stage itself. You'd better hope this show, when it finally starts, is worth my while … because if not, I'm going to give it and you a going-over online that'll make what I did to your husband look like a patta-cake session. What do you say, Ebenezer?" He spun in his chair to face the marionette.

To find that it was less than a foot away from him.

Hetherington leapt to his feet, knocking the chair over in his haste. Involuntarily, he backed away a couple of yards.

"Lampwick? … *LAMPWICK!*"

He glanced overhead, still seeing nothing, and somehow knowing that this was because there was nobody up there.

Yet when he looked at Scrooge again, it was even closer. Still hanging limply on semi-visible wires. But its head was now upright. Its soulless eyes, which were little more than black dots on white greasepaint patches with beetling, bushy brows pasted over the top, had fixed intently on him. For a hair-raising second, that thing that happened with skillfully made and manipulated puppets – that weird illusion that they were actually alive – overtook Hetherington. He half-expected the effigy's hinged jaw to start clacking up and down as a stream of seasonal invective issued out: *"Humbug! Humbug, I say! Every idiot who goes about with 'Merry Christmas' on his lips should be boiled with his own pudding and buried with a stake of holly through his heart!"*

But of course, that didn't happen.

It just hung there, silent, watching him from close up.

Hetherington stared again into the darkened recesses above, craning his neck backward to try and focus on something, anything distinguishable. Seconds passed, but there was no movement up there. Surely if someone was lurking on a gantry, he'd at least hear them? A shuffling … a dull creak of metal?

"Well," he said aloud, belatedly remembering that he had an audience. "It is possible that we're being hoaxed here. It wouldn't be the first time, as you folks are aware. But it's also worth considering that these marionettes are actually nothing to do with Ted Lampwick and the Ambridge Theatre. They're owned by an outside company. And while it's possible that Mr Lampwick may be hanging around in the vicinity, I've seen no sign that anyone else is. And on reflection, I somehow can't picture old Ted – who must be sixty-five easily – climbing up into that roof-space. So, we may also have to consider that this could be a mechanical fault. Perhaps … if the puppet's on runners, if it's all cogs and wheels up there, and the rig hasn't been disassembled yet, this weirdness could be happening by accident. A stiff breeze through a fault in the roof? A gear that keeps slipping?" He paused. "Either way, if I want to establish an explanation, I need to get up there myself."

He stepped around the Scrooge figure, giving it wider berth than perhaps was really necessary, and headed to the wings at stage right. As he went, he glanced backward, half-expecting the marionette to have turned again, its ghoulish painted eyes still fixed on him. But it remained as it had been, facing the knocked-over chair.

"Okay, here we go." Hetherington sidled around the edge of an upright section of flat scenery that was painted with a wintry Dickensian street scene.

Behind it, a narrow path dwindled away between a black brick wall and the rear of several additional flats. The greenish gloom cast by Hetherington's goggles perhaps rendered this thoroughfare spookier than it needed to be. But this wasn't the reason he now hesitated – or so he told himself; he wanted to listen out again. But aside from the faint, shrill moan of wind in the high rafters, there was no other sound in the building. He imagined the snow fluttering relentlessly down outside, blanketing the old industrial-era premises, blotting out the surrounding streets and their rows of dingy terraced houses.

All very Christmassy ... if you believe in that claptrap.

For the first time now, as he ventured behind the flats, he noticed his breath smoking. As Lampwick had said, with the power turned off, the central heating would also be deactivated – and it hadn't taken long for the effect of that to make itself known. Despite Hetherington's earlier bravado when this was mentioned, it would certainly make things uncomfortable. He was well padded, though, and he had a flask of hot coffee in his pack. Even so, he pulled his gloves back on. They were old-fashioned skiing gauntlets and were nice and thick – which would be all the better if this ladder, when he finally found it, proved to be rusty. Not that there was any sign of it. There were lots of ropes back here, either hanging down in front of him or tied off on steel hooks in the wall, but nothing else. It was bare and basic behind the scenery, the air reeking of sawdust and fresh paint. How often that magical theatrical fantasy was shattered when you poked your nose round the back and saw how functional the reality was.

He progressed along the passage until he reached the top of another back-stair, which descended into murk. There was no point going under the stage again, but from this position he was able to see past the rearmost gap in the flats and across to the far wings. The ladder might be over there – but then a shadowy form flitted past a space between two opposing bits of scenery

It was a brief second. No more than a flicker of movement, and then it was gone. But it was all Hetherington needed.

"Ah … hah." He felt both irritated and elated. "Caught you."

He held his breath for several heartbeats. Nothing else happened, but it didn't matter – he knew what he'd seen. Sliding quickly out along the wall painted with the image of Old London Town, he broke into a run as he crossed the stage, not just adrenalized by the scent of a foe but by the prospect of what a chase and catch would do to his viewing figures. The excited rasp of his breath and scuffing of his feet could no doubt be heard throughout the theatre, but speed was all. He was onto something big here. This one might even travel beyond the confines of the internet. A TV slot, perhaps the local news …

… would be just the shot in the arm that Fear Itself needed.

He reached stage-left and slotted himself through the gap between the flats. Again, he was in a cramped world of props, ropes and sawdust.

"I know you're here!" he said loudly, blundering towards the stage front.

But now there was no sign of anyone.

The Victorian arch appeared on his left, while on his right there was a large pair of double-doors. They were painted black, which might explain why he hadn't noticed them when making his earlier round-trip with Lampwick. They were also heavy and crude; they looked more like barn doors, though a notice on the left one read:

Workshop

Hetherington barged at the doors with his shoulder. As expected, they held firm. Something else he'd be taking up with his host in the morning. "*All* parts of the theatre except the bar and the office!" he growled. "That was the deal!"

He glanced through the arch onto the stage. Nothing out there had changed; the hanging figure of Scrooge was exactly as he'd left it, although … was it possible it had pivoted around again? From its previous angle it should have been shoulder-on, but as always seemed to be the case now, it was facing him. However, this time he wasn't concerned, not now he *knew* there was somebody else here.

With a slow, dull creak, what sounded like a door opened behind him …

Briefly, Hetherington froze. For the first time in his many years of ghost hunts and exposés, the proverbial chill ran up his spine. Then he spun.

The workshop stood ajar.

"That's impossible," he said under his breath, momentarily breaking one of his own cardinal rules by lending credence to the illogical. "I tried those doors. They were locked." Despite the deepening chill, he mopped more sweat from his brow. "Unless, of course," he licked his lips, which conversely were bone-dry, "these doors were locked from the other side … by someone who must still be in there."

And yet now, for some reason, has unlocked them again?

Though this was an invitation he surely couldn't refuse – in fact mustn't, given what his audience would think – he actually wondered if he should. Fleetingly, he wondered what he was even doing in this cold, dark, tomb-like building when he could have been at home in the warmth, kicking back on the sofa with Marsha.

"Because we're here to unravel what's real from what's unreal," he said, forcefully answering his own question. "We are here to undermine the phonies and the frauds, and tonight perhaps we're going to nab the biggest fish of all: the annual fallacious farce that is Christmas."

He pushed at the workshop doors.

They swung in onto a surprisingly cavernous interior, though it was also cluttered with awkward-shaped objects: workbenches, trestle-tables, tools, bits of timber and hardboard. On all sides there were more flats, decked with garish imagery, either lying in stacks or leaning against the walls. And then there was something else.

Right in the middle of the room, on the floor, was his hi-tech Acorn Trail-Cam. A hundred quid's worth of motion-sensitive night vision. Now in several pieces.

Hetherington strode forward and gazed down at it dumbly. In the green twilight, it was difficult to tell whether it had been disassembled or smashed. But the mere fact it had been removed from where he'd positioned it below-stairs, and brought up here …

Another chill crept through his bones. "I … I …"

The inside of his mouth was as dry as his lips. He couldn't give voice to what he felt.

People always try to pull the wool over my eyes, but this is the first time anyone's attacked my stuff …

He turned stiffly, almost indignantly scanning the room. Again, there was no sign that anyone was in here. There wasn't even a place where a person could hide.

Except for in the farthest corner, maybe twenty yards away, where yet another stack of flats had been propped against the north-facing wall, leaving a shadow-filled gap between itself and the east-facing wall. It was only a narrow gap, the depth and breadth of a coffin – but still sufficient to conceal someone.

He walked over there with a slow, deliberate tread, accidentally kicking over a tin of paint, which clattered as it rolled, splurging a green puddle across the bare floorboards.

"Shit!" he hissed, though it was hardly a disaster. As he'd already seen, it was a utilitarian world back here. Besides, they owed him a camera.

The corner of the flats stood right in front of him, the black recess behind them just out of sight. "It's your last chance to come clean," he said. "Fail to do that, and you'll be outed … to the whole world."

Still there was no sound

"Despite what you've done to my gear, there's nothing personal in this. If we can make good on the cost of that, there'll be no hard feelings."

Still no response.

"I warn you, exposing frauds is my trade. My reason to live."

Still nothing.

Without further warning, Hetherington stepped around the corner. "It's my …"

The figure waiting there startled him for all kinds of horrible reasons, not least its lugubrious frown and lifeless, painted eyes. But mainly because the last time he'd seen it, it had been downstairs. It was Marley's Ghost. Not sitting now, but standing upright against the rear wall, its head no longer drooping and the bandage that had supported its jaw now absent.

"It's my …" Hetherington stammered again.

Was this the same marionette? He noted the unstitched tear in the left shoulder of its frockcoat. Had someone carried it up here? Along with his camera? Why in God's name exert all this effort just to perpetrate a hoax? Or was it a costume?

Can that be it? Is this someone dressed up?

Dazedly, he reached out to touch the thing.

"It's my, my ..."

His fingers made tentative contact with the figure's bare, wooden cranium. It was hard, hollow.

"My business."

Abruptly, its jaw clacked downward, the vivid red gash of its mouth extending all the way to its breastbone.

"BUSINESS!" a distant voice shrieked in the back of Hetherington's memory.

The next thing he knew he was stumbling away across the workshop. Aside from the jaw, he'd never seen the thing move. Not once, not at all. He told himself this over and over. And yet now, even though he could hear sounds behind him – that paint-pot clattering and rolling again, as if something had kicked it while coming after him – he refused to look back.

"There'll be an explanation," he chuntered. "There always is. It's a trick, a charade."

The workshop doors swam into view, and beyond those the Victorian arch. But now another figure was standing there, blocking it. It wore a nightcap and dressing gown, and its luminous eyes peered at him from under bristly tufts of eyebrow.

Hetherington screamed.

It was the first time he'd made this sound in adulthood. He made it again a second later, involuntarily, as he blundered towards the rear of the wings. There was another door back there somewhere; he'd seen it earlier – but where? Dear God, the sense of pursuit was intolerable. Then the door slammed into him with a stunning blow, both body and face. Refusing to yield to dizziness, he yanked it open and all but leapt down the back-stair beyond, fighting his way through the maze of backstage passages, sending another of his stationary cameras crashing to the floor but ignoring it, scrabbling madly this way and that until, more by accident than design, he reached the basement bar.

"What the hell are you running for?" he raved at himself as he dashed across it. "They're puppets, that's all. *Bloody puppets!*"

Even so, he didn't risk a glance into the far corner where the puppet of the Ghost of Christmas Past had been seated, despite a distinct impression gained through his peripheral vision that a figure in white was no longer sitting over there but *standing*.

He all but flew the remaining distance to the fire-exit door next to the electrics cupboard, only to open it and find himself blinded by swirling flakes, and when they briefly cleared, gazing up a flight of snow-carpeted steps to a tall, wrought-iron gate now bound closed with a length of heavy chain.

A chain?

That damn horror in the workshop! I knew there was something missing!

It didn't matter. Ducking back inside, Hetherington crossed the lower section of bar to the foot of the stair leading up to the lobby. But he'd only half ascended this when he saw that yet another figure was waiting at the top, an immense shape in heavy winter robes, with a wig and fake beard, and a holly wreath on its head.

Sweating and whimpering, he tottered back the way he'd come. It would mean chancing the upper bar again, which he did, at breakneck speed, again refusing to glance into the far corner, though the white form he'd glimpsed over there was much closer, before crashing shoulder-first through the anteroom and then back through the backstage area, still declining to look left or right, turning corner after corner, at any second expecting some horrific, limbering form to manifest from the gloom and wrap its wooden arms around him, but instead colliding with more of his own equipment, an ultra-expensive EMF monitor exploding as it was hammered to the floor.

So bloody what?

At last reaching the short upward stair, Hetherington staggered through the old stage-door and into the tiled exit passage leading to the rear of the building.

He was still wearing his night-vision goggles, but that opaque patch of blackness at the far end of his escape route remained unchanged.

"It looks menacing," Lampwick said. Too bloody right it does!

But it was the only way out, and anyway, a growing sense that something again was close behind was the final spur. Yelling incoherently, the ghost hunter charged down the passage, rushing headlong into the blackness at its farthest extremity.

Initially, he assumed the fabric that swirled around him was a curtain or drape, perhaps a draft-excluder at the outer door. But good God, there was so much of it, and it was so black and heavy, and it smelled so foul. And holy Jesus, Mary and Joseph, there was something else in here alongside him. Something hiding. Or maybe not hiding, *waiting*.

As it had been waiting all along.

Inside this colossal costume …

"Jesus God in Heaven!" Hetherington shrieked as an object shimmered into view in front of his face, a glinting crescent of steel: the cold, curved perfection of a razor-edged scythe.

*

"Quite a bit of expensive kit in there," said the lad in jumper and jeans, as he brought another of the marionettes outside. "Some of it looks damaged, mind."

"Damaged?" Lampwick enquired, chugging on one of the fat King Edward cigars his granddaughter had given him for Christmas. He presumed the lad was referring to all those cameras and monitors and such. He hadn't noticed that any of it was broken, though he hadn't looked too closely. It was certainly all over the place.

"Only a couple of pieces," the lad said. "Most of it's all right. There's even a pair of night-vision goggles. Reckon they cost a bit."

"The bloke who left it behind left *that* too." Lampwick nodded down the snowy street at the rear of the theatre. At its far end, a day and two nights' worth of soft white flakes were heaped on the roof and bonnet of a parked Subaru Impreza. "He was supposed to take it all away on Christmas morning, but when I got here, he'd gone without it."

The lad threw the puppet into the back of the colourfully illustrated van. This was the one dressed as Scrooge. Up close, in the bright white snow-light of a Boxing Day morning, it was easier to see how plain it actually was: with its wires removed, it was a jointed wooden mannequin, nothing more, and now that its greasepaint and make-up had been smeared away, it was grey in colour, almost featureless.

"Wouldn't fancy leaving a motor like that around here … no offence," the lad said as he headed back into the building.

"None taken." Lampwick puffed on his cigar. "This corner of town's not quite what it was. But you're right; he was obviously a more casual sort than I thought. He didn't even put the power back on before he left. I've no idea where he is at present."

"Probably sleeping off a hangover, eh?" the lad said, reappearing with another marionette under his arm. This one was clad as the Ghost of Christmas Past. Again, it looked like nothing in broad daylight, Lampwick thought. It was amazing what this Ms Mordrake and her Magic Puppet Theatre could do.

"I doubt that, somehow," he said. "Anyway, he'll show up. So … Ms Mordrake didn't fancy coming to collect the stuff herself?"

"Nah. Pays an oik like me to do that." The lad headed back inside. "I don't mind. I'm on double-time today."

Lampwick glanced through the open doors at the back of the van, and saw four of the figures that had entertained the local children so royally during December: Scrooge and the three Spirits of the Season, nothing more now than a heap of disorderly wooden parts, their costumes just messy rags. No doubt, once they got home, they'd be stripped down and cleaned, maybe dressed as pirates or angels or pantomime characters, or who knew what at this time of year. At the far end of the vehicle's interior, a fifth dusty figure was propped against the wheel arch. Lampwick couldn't see much of it, just an outline – but this one hadn't even been dressed in a costume. He extricated his cigar and leaned forward, gazing into the dim interior. Surely there was something about it? But then the lad asked him to mind out, and threw in the last of the marionettes, Marley's Ghost. It struck the figure by the wheel arch with a *clack*, causing it to shift lifelessly and its left arm to flop into the daylight.

It was nothing, Lampwick realised. Wood, like all the others.

Not real.

KRAMPUS

Grandpa Ludwig didn't usually participate on Christmas Day when we all gathered around the fire after dinner and urged the adults to tell ghost stories. Part of the time it was because he was asleep, but also, I think, it was because he didn't enjoy such things. We all knew he'd had a difficult time as a child. It's not everyone who can boast that his father was condemned in absentia to die by the guillotine, even if he did live to tell the tale, but Grandpa Ludwig was of such an age by this time – seventy-five at least – that he surely had no real memories of those dark and deadly days. In addition, his father had been a great storyteller, an author of children's fiction as famous in Germany at one time as Enid Blyton was in England, so it hardly seemed possible that Grandpa Ludwig had not inherited at least a smidgen of that talent.

As such, one year, when it was plain that Grandpa Ludwig was wide awake after dinner, laughing uproariously with the other adults, mince pie in hand, paper crown perched at a jaunty angle on his balding pate, we urged him to start off the annual ghost story game by telling us one of his own. Grandpa was very thoughtful for a moment or two. He took a sip of port wine, before nodding gravely and saying that, yes, it was time he told us all his ghost story.

His choice of phrase quite surprised me. The notion that, all along, he'd possessed a ghost story that was exclusively his own, and that for so many years he'd been withholding it – who knew for what reason? – was an eerie and mysterious concept.

I remember how we youngsters huddled together on the carpet in front of the fire, legs crossed, and how my mum turned the lights down, as she always did on this occasion, leaving only the faint glow of the candles on the Christmas cake and the orange embers in the hearth to reflect our rapt attention. Grandpa Ludwig took off his spectacles, polished them with his handkerchief, and then pinched the bridge of his nose, a sure sign I would later learn that the event he was about to recount came from memory, not imagination.

This is what he told us …

*

Most of you will know that my father and his brother, Klaus, were not identical twins, but that they *were* twins and as children they were so alike that many people could not tell them apart. Of course, in terms of temperament and personality, they could not have been more different.

My own recollections of Uncle Klaus are that he was more physically imposing than my father; he was tall and athletically built, with shining blond hair and piercing blue eyes. A more idealised Aryan male there could not have been, though I didn't understand that philosophy at the time. Nor did I really notice how relations between my father and his brother, while not exactly hostile, were never better than cool. At least, that was always the case during my lifetime. Of course, I knew nothing about my father's refusal to join the Hitler Youth in 1927, which had meant that my family – Uncle Klaus's family, more to the point – was regarded with suspicion for a brief time.

The one thing about Uncle Klaus I didn't like was the scar on his left cheek. It was not a particularly awful one, little more than a horizontal white line, but even to my childhood eyes, it gave him a colder, crueller aspect. Apparently it had been caused when he'd run into a barbed wire fence while playing outdoors as a toddler, but he was always rather proud of it, or so my father would later say, telling anyone who asked that it was a duelling scar, as if he was the scion of a Prussian aristocrat rather than the son of a small-town Bavarian solicitor.

The last time I ever saw Uncle Klaus was in 1939, and though I was still very young, I had some vague notion that Germany was on the eve of war. He was wearing a uniform when he came to see us. Many times in the past he'd been in uniform – uniforms were quite commonplace in those days – but this one was jet black and it sported the SS Sig Runes on its collar and the *Totenkopf*, or Death's Head, as they would call it here in England, on its armband. I don't think Uncle Klaus had come with the express intention of warning my father that he was in imminent danger, but I was sent to my room while the adults discussed matters, and so fierce was the resulting argument that I heard it through the floorboards. Snatches of that dispute still remain in my memory.

"Will you continue writing fairy stories while the world burns, Eric?" my uncle demanded to know.

"What does it matter if I do?" my father replied.

"It matters if they call you 'traitor' for it."

"Never once have I written or spoken a word of treason."

"Nor have you written against it. Is it not the case that, several times now, you have been invited to supply poems, ballads and books in honour of our cause, and have always refused? We stand on the brink of a great destiny, and yet you – a man of widespread influence – seem determined to disapprove of it."

"Klaus, I am not a political writer."

"Eric, not everyone agrees with that …"

Before Uncle Klaus finally left, I came to the top of the stairs in tears. I might have been a child, but I was not a fool; I knew the sound of irreparable damage when I heard it. He glanced up as he pulled his hat down over his brow and climbed into his long leather coat; his expression was one of deep regret, but also bitter anger and betrayal. He spoke to me, but I was in too anguished a state at the time to make sense of his words.

We left our home the very next day, not just our house, but Germany itself. I have almost no memory of that rushed dawn departure as I apparently slept through most of it.

*

Grandpa Ludwig sipped his port.

The mood had turned rapidly and unexpectedly sombre. His family's narrow escape from Nazi

Germany had never been the easiest topic of conversation. His writer father, though he'd adopted England as his new abode, had been haunted to the end of his days by his inability to reconcile himself with a homeland whose history and culture he had loved but which had been subverted to such a ghastly degree that he no longer knew it when he left. Grandpa Ludwig, of course, had barely experienced Germany. He now had only the faintest discernible accent, and though his early days were undoubtedly difficult – a boy named Weidmann living in post-war Britain! – he soon adapted to his new home and in time became as English as Winston Churchill.

Perhaps this was why, after another contemplative sip or two, he was able to continue with his narrative. Though his mood was no lighter. Far from it …

*

We must move forward now, to the Christmas Eve of 1948.

To an eleven-year-old those pre-war days already seemed a receding memory, but the good times had not yet returned. Britain was a land of food rationing, bombed cities and bereaved families. Ironically, though my family were immigrants, our position was better than some. My father had learned to speak English, but never to a standard where he might write in that tongue, at least not with the same eloquence he'd shown when writing in German. However, he was able to teach, so we had regular money and a reasonably comfortable home in the suburbs. My two best friends at the time were Billy Flynn and Peter Osgood, boys from the same road in which I lived and fellow pupils at the Catholic school I attended. Both their fathers had fought in the war, and survived – one had even been present at the relief of Belsen – so to them any German who'd annoyed the Nazis to the point where they'd driven him into exile was someone to be admired. Hence, they never treated me like an outsider.

Hard though youngsters may find it to believe now, on the Christmas Eve in question we were required to attend school as if it were any normal day. We had a two-week holiday, but it only commenced the following morning on Christmas Day. For all that, our teachers were kind enough to release us at lunchtime, so Billy, Peter and I took the opportunity to divert through the town centre on our way home. There was a raw, wintry feel that afternoon. The snow that had fallen the previous week had thawed a little, but had later frozen again, and great, dirty mounds of it were now piled at the end of each pavement. The gutters and bus shelters sparkled with icicles; white frost covered every branch and blade of grass. We were well wrapped in our coats and scarves; we had our balaclavas and our woollen mittens. Even so, there is only so much one can do to fend off that depth of cold, but we were determined to endure it because a great treat awaited us.

The English version of our German Saint Nikolaus is of course Father Christmas. They share much in common. Both are fat, jolly men with white curls and white beards. They wear warm winter robes and dispense presents to good children. However, there are some differences. In Germany, Saint Nikolaus would visit homes on the eve of December 6, whereas in England, Father Christmas would visit on Christmas Eve itself. While Saint Nikolaus bore ecclesial accoutrements – for instance, he wore a mitre and carried a crosier – the English Father Christmas had a druidic air; there was something in his makeup of the old spirit of winter, which, looking on it as an adult, seems almost pagan to me. But even so, in England, as in Germany, children were taught that this benign figure was a saint, beloved of Christ, so his magical gifts were to be welcomed and adored. As a small side-matter … in Germany, St. Nikolaus had a shadowy other-self, little known and an entirely dissimilar personality. But more about him later.

The purpose of our diversion into the centre of town that Christmas Eve afternoon was concerned neither with Saint Nikolaus nor Father Christmas, but in fact with Santa Claus, their American counterpart, newly introduced to the United Kingdom in the aftermath of the war. Santa Claus, though in many ways indistinguishable from his European brethren, had one very unique attribute: he could actually be spoken to. He would sit children on his knee, and they could request their presents face-to-face. I'm talking of course about the famous department store Santa Claus, who had been a fixture in American cities since the turn of the century, and now at last had come to Britain.

The department store in question was *Halley & Meredith's*, whose palatial residence was in the very centre of our town, in a space, if I recall correctly, which is now occupied by a wine bar, a Poundstretcher and a kebab shop. At the time we referred to *Halley & Meredith's* as 'posh', though in truth it would probably have seemed fairly second rate compared to Harrods in London or Kendals in Manchester. But it occupied a great baroque building, and its frontal canopy was hung with international flags. It even had its own taxi rank outside, the implication being that the sort of people who shopped at *Halley & Meredith's* could easily afford to take cabs rather than having to get the bus. One entered the premises through revolving doors, assuming that the concierge on duty – a dapper chap with a military air, wearing a shell grey overcoat with gold braid at its shoulders – would permit you access. Under normal circumstances it seemed highly possible that three schoolboys lacking the governance of their parents would be refused, but this was Christmas Eve, and everyone was excited and in a good mood, and in any case, Santa Claus was waiting inside.

Or was it Father Christmas or Saint Nikolaus? Or someone else?

Halley & Meredith's seemed vast and crowded that day; we trekked past *Scarves, Gloves And Hats*, past *Cosmetics*, past *Haberdashery*, past *Men's Tailoring*, past *Ladies' Shoes*, all locations which, when I'd been present with my mother, had signified hours of tedium. But now, to see them decked with tinsel and boughs of evergreen was almost too much for an eleven-year-old to take – our sense of thrill rose inexorably, and of course we still had the 'Christmas Grotto' at the end of it all. We finally found this hallowed place down at the basement level, a venue normally reserved for tools and gardening equipment, though now it had become a magical kingdom.

In hindsight, it had probably been done quite cheaply, but we walked along a side-aisle which we no longer recognised, passing under arches made of pine branches and hung with multi-coloured Chinese lanterns. Streamers and paper chains were looped across the ceiling. Christmas trees stood on each counter, decked with ornaments and fairy lights. Cotton wool had been laid over racks of goods to imitate snow. In the drab, grey Britain of those immediate post-war years, it was a delightful thing to behold. Even the shop assistants, those straight-backed ladies who always teetered around *Halley & Meredith's* in tight skirts and tall heels, looking beautiful but severe, seemed so much more human in green conical 'elf' hats, and also because they were smiling and chattering brightly.

Santa Claus himself was quite remarkable. A knee-high white picket fence woven with holly had closed off a small area, and he was in the middle of it, seated on a throne-like chair. He wore the traditional crimson robe trimmed with white fur, and it flowed out around him on all sides; it was far too large to be practical – one could never have walked around in such a garment. Beneath it, he wore a bottle-green waistcoat, crimson pantaloons and black boots, again trimmed with white fur. Of course, he had a capacious belly and a thick white beard, which fell almost to his belt-buckle. To complete the picture, there were oodles of gift-wrapped presents stacked behind him, as if he was ready right now to load his sleigh and depart on his goodly mission.

There was a hubbub of excitement from the queueing youngsters, most of whom were there with their mothers and grandmothers, or both. It may seem strange now, three eleven-year-olds waiting to see Santa Claus in a department store, but we weren't the eldest there. Other older children were also present, patiently waiting their turn, eyes fixed with wonder on the resplendent figure. World War Two, with its prolonged loss of life, property and innocence and then the drudgery and austerity that had followed, was entirely responsible for this. In some ways we were older than our age back then, but in others we were much younger.

Of course, when Santa's hearty laughter finally told us our turn had come, we older children didn't actually sit on the big man's knee. We advanced through the gate in the wicket fence and stood there politely, hands behind our backs, as he addressed us.

"And what do we have here?" he said, his blue eyes twinkling. In keeping with the myth that he hailed from some frozen Tyrolean land, he spoke with a central European accent. "Three young men, in whose steady hands the future of the world must reside."

Peter, always the boldest among us, answered first when we were asked what we were hoping to obtain at Christmas.

"I would like a new bicycle, sir," he said soberly, as if he knew that he really was asking for quite a lot and that such an extravagant gift might be beyond even Santa Claus's ability to bestow.

"A new bicycle, hmmm," our host rumbled. "We'll have to see about that, but who knows?, anything is possible." He switched his attention to Billy. "And for you, young sir?"

"I would like a toy gun and holster, sir," Billy said. "Like you see on the cowboy films. Maybe a cowboy hat as well?"

"Hmmm … well, a hat and a gun. Those are quite the sort of items a young man should possess, though you won't be meeting many Red Indians here in Lancashire, I shouldn't think."

"No, sir," Billy said in a tone which suggested he'd given this matter weighty consideration but was still set on his course.

"Hmmm … well, this is all to the good, gentlemen. Such manly gifts will prepare you for the trials of adulthood."

This conversation might have seemed a little more protracted than most of those Santa Claus had engaged in up until now, and yet he still didn't turn to me – and frankly I wasn't concerned in the least. Because from the moment I'd set eyes upon him up close, I was struck with the kind of horror that even back in the war-ravaged 1940s most people would experience only once in a lifetime.

It was Uncle Klaus.

That is all I can say.

Feel free not to believe me, but I swear to you it is the absolute truth.

He'd changed enormously. Beneath that thick, white beard and the rosy cheeks – the former of which was clearly real, the latter fake – he was as gaunt as a leper: his skin had a yellowish tinge; his eyes, which were neither as blue nor as twinkly as I'd first thought, were sunken in skullish cavities; his lips were thin and covered with cracks and sores. But there was no mistaking that horizontal scar on his left cheek, even though many other scars had appeared since. And now at last he turned to me, and he pointed with a long, bony finger, the nail at the end of which was sharp and twisting.

"And for you, Ludwig?" he said, though it wasn't really a question. "Krampus … ja?"

"I … I just want to go home," I stuttered.

"Nein!" he said harshly, wagging that terrible finger in admonition and fixing me with a stare so malevolent that it was all I could do not to faint. *"Krampus!"*

The next thing I knew, we were being ushered away down another aisle by one of the elf-ladies, and Peter and Billy were gossiping excitedly about whether or not they had increased their chances of receiving their much sought-for presents. In their eyes at least, nothing unusual had happened, and when I glanced back over my shoulder at the diminishing form of Santa Claus in his golden grotto, a little girl was positioned on his knee, shivering with delight as he cuddled her and crooned a carol, and the queue of other children awaiting their own turn had extended until it snaked down the entire length of the department store's basement.

When we emerged outside, it was turning dark and tiny spots of snow were spiralling down. There were many more people about, attending to their last-minute shopping, and the roads were a chaos of vans, wagons and cars. My two friends were still in a state of exhilaration as we commenced the long walk home, so it was difficult broaching the subject of whether or not they'd thought there was something strange about the man masquerading as Santa Claus in *Halley & Meredith's*. Clearly, neither had detected anything. Peter did acknowledge that I'd seemed a little tongue-tied when Santa Claus had spoken to me, though he hadn't noticed the man address me by my own name, and certainly recalled nothing about his use of the term 'Krampus'.

Not that they would have known what it meant, anyway. Not that anyone in this country would have known. You see, Krampus was the name given to that shadowy other-self of Saint Nikolaus, the one I referred to earlier. Whereas in English-speaking lands, Father Christmas and Santa Claus have always preferred to ignore naughty children, in Germanic countries Krampus actively punishes them. I had seen illustrations of him in children's books written by my father, and he is truly grotesque; a monster, a deformed devil with horns, hooves and a humped back. The sack he carries is not intended for the provision of gifts, but to abduct those misbehaving youths he encounters on his travels, and to carry them back to his lair where all manner of torments will be inflicted on them. You look shocked. Don't be. In the days of my youth, children were to be seen and not heard. Parents, while loving, were stern. There was a price to pay for transgression. Bad behaviour was never tolerated.

Even now, it pains me to recollect that journey home from the shops. I was so distressed by what had happened that I contributed almost nothing to my friends' joyous jabber. All of a sudden, Christmas – the culmination of so many weeks' eager anticipation, the date we had ached for since the onset of winter – meant nothing to me. The ruddy glow of Yule candles in passing windows, the falling snow – now a thickening, shimmering cascade – should have rendered a perfect setting. But my thoughts were in turmoil. More than once I glanced over my shoulder, especially after we left the town centre and entered the residential districts, where doors were closed, curtains drawn and fellow pedestrians little more than occasional muffled shadows. Though I never saw anything amiss, I was increasingly certain that someone was keeping pace with us just beyond the range of our vision.

At last the moment came when we were to go our different ways. We stopped beneath a corner streetlamp, Peter and Billy pumping my hand, clapping my shoulder, wishing me all the best for the season.

"A little touch of Germany for you tonight, Ludwig," Peter said.

"What do you mean?" I demanded, even more unnerved.

"This!" he said, smiling, indicating the snow. "We get this now and then at Christmas, but in Germany you get it every year, or so I'm told."

"Not every year," I replied, still shaken.

"Happy Christmas anyway, Ludwig!" they shouted as they walked away, leaving me alone in the lamplight, flakes swirling past. I looked again over my shoulder.

The street we had just walked along was lined down either side with terraced houses; a perfectly normal street in our part of the world, yet now an increasingly stiff breeze was whipping the snow in eddies; on some occasions I could see as far along it as the coal wagon parked at its distant end, on others no more than thirty yards. I remained there for several minutes, convinced there'd be something to fix on if only I could gaze into the murk hard enough. Intermittently down that street, curtains were only half-drawn, thus allowing rays of soft, warm lamplight to penetrate outward. Without warning, someone passed one of these. I blinked – and they'd gone again, hidden by renewed swirls of flakes. But it was someone headed in my direction. Someone wearing red.

It could have been any ordinary person walking home; there was absolutely no need to assume the worst. But briefly I was rooted in place. Only slowly, with great difficulty, was I able to retreat to the edge of the pavement, where again I waited. I don't know why; it makes no sense now – it was as if I had some inner urgent need to *know* I was in danger rather than simply fear it. But then something happened that leant genuine panic to my heels. I spied the figure again, much closer this time – maybe forty yards away – crossing the street to the side on which I was waiting. It was only a silhouette, half-glimpsed as it passed through another shaft of flake-speckled lamplight, but it was bent forward in ungainly fashion, its back humped, its heavy robes trailing behind it.

There was no further debate in my mind. I spun around and raced blindly along the next street, and along the one after that, regardless of the treacherous footing. I must have covered half the distance home before I stopped to get my breath. I had seen no-one else that whole way, but likewise no-one was in sight behind me either, and now, the flakes having relented a little, I was able to see a good distance in every direction – and spied nothing but snow-covered road junctions, the red-brick gable walls of houses, the weak palls of light cast by streetlamps. Nothing advanced through them, so I felt a little better, though I had yet to cross Dalewood Brow. That place no longer exists today – a supermarket and offices have been built there instead, but in my childhood it consisted of several hundred yards of derelict colliery land, hummocky and deeply overgrown; a wonderful place for children to play in summer, but in wintry darkness a test of anyone's nerve. Especially on this occasion.

I didn't need to go over the Brow. If I turned left at this point, I could just as easily walk around it, making my way home via lamp-lit streets, passing more houses, more cars. Yet that would take much longer – maybe add half an hour to my journey, and all at once I wanted desperately to be home, if for no other reason than my fingers were frozen and my feet turning numb. So, I pushed open the creaky gate in the wrought iron fence that ran along the Brow's edge, and set off hurriedly up its winding, cindery path. Because the Brow was covered with snow, much more of it was visible to me than I'd expected, and somehow that was comforting.

All the way I glanced nervously around, able to see a vast expanse of white, broken only by the occasional black skeletons of trees, or protruding twists of frosty underbrush.

I quickly lost sight of the wrought iron fence, but my confidence was growing that I would soon be home. I was approaching the Hump, as we knew it; a great slagheap with a foot-tunnel driven through it. Beyond that I needed only to cross the canal bridge and ascend a footpath through thickets to the edge of the housing estate on which I lived. That was when I heard the distant *creak* of the gate.

Did I actually hear it? Was it possible to hear anything in that situation? The gate was dozens and dozens of yards behind me. My ears were muffled by the balaclava. Even if I had heard it, might it not have been shifted by a gust of wind? I couldn't see far enough back in this twilit snowy realm to be sure one way or the other, but then I heard something else – the steady *crunch* of approaching feet.

I didn't wait to hear more. I ran on up the remainder of the path and through the foot-tunnel. This in itself – a straight low corridor of damp brick, completely unlit, running for at least fifty yards – would be a nightmare in the modern age, but notions of 'stranger-danger' were almost unheard of in that long-ago era. I was nearly home; this foot-tunnel was part of my normal world; I had no fear of it – until this point. Because though I got through to the other side without hindrance, I stopped again, for no good reason I can think of now, and peered back, and to my utmost shock I beheld a figure entering the tunnel from the other side. Again it was nothing more than a silhouette framed on the moon-lit snow, but, as before, it was hunched forward – so much so that

I couldn't see its head, and it moved with a heavy, shambling gait; immense, unwieldy robes dragged behind it. The clomping of its footfalls on the stony ground echoed along the passage towards me; those sounds were like no impacts of shoes or boots that I'd ever heard.

I simply fled. Raw terror drove me across the canal bridge at reckless speed – it had no safety barriers and was shod with ice, yet I careered over it like a madman. The path beyond led uphill through tangled, snow-clad thickets. There were any number of places where an assailant might lie in wait and leap out, but I bypassed them all without a glance. Even when I left the Brow and ran along the next street to my own, I was pursued by inexorable fear, which only intensified as I rounded the corner onto the final straight. I had a nagging certainty that I'd be grabbed at the death.

I wasn't, but worse was to follow.

With sobs of relief, I kicked open our garden gate and ran up the path. The front door was locked, so I veered left, running down the side alley past our allotment and coal bunker, to the kitchen door. To my disbelief, this was locked too. I fumbled wildly under the scullery window, found our spare key, and let myself in, slamming the door closed behind me. The next thing I noticed was the cold supper waiting on the kitchen table – some boiled bacon, bread and jam, a mug of milk – with a handwritten letter alongside it. Though the house was luxuriously warm, coals burning in both the kitchen stove and behind the fireguard on the grate in the living room, a new kind of chill struck me.

My parents were out.

I knew that before I even snatched up the note and began to read. It was from my father, and it explained that he and my mother had been invited round by neighbours for a Christmas Eve sherry. They would only be a couple of hours.

But which neighbours? He didn't specify.

And when had this couple of hours commenced? Was it shortly to expire or did it still stretch before me?

I yanked off my balaclava, my hair soaked with icy sweat – and heard a distinctive *clank* as the front gate banged open again. Incredulously, I listened to the progression of heavy misshapen feet along our snowy front path, and then into the alley beside the house, whereupon they abruptly stopped. I was now listening so intently that I fancied I could hear the whispering of the snowflakes outside, but apart from that there was only silence. Torturous, prolonged silence.

It is almost impossible to convey the horror and isolation I felt at that moment, even though I was ensconced in my own home. I stared fixedly at the kitchen door. For a time, there was nothing else in the world but that door – and what I suspected lurked just beyond it. I was unable to move; I didn't *dare* move, terrified that if my feet scuffed on the floor they would alert the thing to my presence, even though such thoughts were patently ludicrous – it had followed me all the way home. Even if it hadn't, it knew where I lived; according to our myths, it knew where every child lived.

There was a soft crunch of snow, this directly on the other side of the door, and then a further pause. Was it listening in through the planks as I was listening out? We had a telephone – I don't know why it never occurred to me to run and dial 999. I suspect I was simply too mesmerised by events. My nerves were taut as cello strings, my hair standing on end. But I quickly broke from this stupor when the door-handle started to turn.

I think I may have screamed aloud as I lurched forward and rammed home the upper bolt. Immediately, the handle ceased moving. There was another prolonged silence. I stood rigid, eyes goggling, awaiting the next move. Then the handle turned again, this time with violence, and there was a long, dull groan as a significant weight was pressed against the door from the other side. I was far from confident the single bolt would hold, especially when the weight was withdrawn and, instead, a heavy blow landed. Followed by another blow and another; loud, echoing reports, increasingly angry, which must have been heard all along our street. The kitchen door was solid oak, but it shook and shook, and I imagined that its screws would flirt from their moorings under such an assault.

It was a sure sign of how enthralled by fear I was that only now did it strike me to drive home the lower bolt as well. At first this was difficult: the assailant was hammering on the woodwork, not just with hands but with feet like iron clubs, and the lower section of the door vibrated so hard that it rarely lined up with the jamb – so hard that I thought it would shatter inward – but at last I managed to slide the bolt into its mount, and then ram my key into the lock and turn that too. All violence without instantly ceased.

The silence that followed this was perhaps the worst part of it, for all I could do was hover there in a state of near-paralysis, unsure whether my unwanted visitor had slunk off into the night, or was still present, contemplating another means of ingress. When I suddenly heard a *clunk* of metal at the front of the house, I shrieked hoarsely and stumbled through into our entrance hall, but not without first taking my mother's rolling pin from one of the kitchen worktops. I still remember vividly how that hall seemed to elongate before me, to telescope out to inordinate length as I stood at the kitchen end and peered down it, past the evergreens draped over the stair banister, past the telephone table, past the wooden coat stand, to the front door itself, which, even as I watched, began to open.

I dashed down there with rolling pin raised, like some fearless warrior, screaming. But I was actually on my last legs, and I tripped on the rug before I got there and found myself pitching forward – into the arms of my astonished father.

Neither he nor my mother could speak they were so taken by surprise, but it soon became clear to them from my flow of semi-delirious gibberish that I was not playing some silly game. Despite my pleas that he lock all the doors and call for police assistance, my father went promptly down the side alley to the rear of the house. He found nobody lurking there, but with the aid of a candle, he noted extensive damage to our kitchen door. Afterwards, he listened again to the tale I had to tell him, and I left nothing out – but though he turned a trifle pale at my mention of the department store Santa Claus who'd appeared to know me and looked like Uncle Klaus, I don't think he really believed that part of it.

Though I was eleven years old, I spent that Christmas Eve in my parents' bed, alongside my mother. My father slept in the armchair downstairs, next to the fire, which he stoked up to a good blaze before switching off the lights. Apparently, he spent an uncomfortable but undisturbed night, and never once relinquished his grip on the poker. By morning, a fresh snowfall had obliterated all traces of footprints on our property. In a strange way, I was quite glad of that – I had no desire to see the shape of those left by our Christmas Eve intruder.

*

Grandpa Ludwig lapsed into distant memory as he sipped his port wine.

"Surely there was some kind of investigation?" my dad finally asked. Clearly, this was the first time he'd ever heard this particular story.

Grandpa Ludwig nodded. "Absolutely. At the first opportunity my father sought out the general manager of *Halley & Meredith's* to officially complain that their Santa Claus had frightened me, and that he might well be the same person who had followed me home. Even the police became involved, and the Santa Claus in question – his name was William Harrison, and he was an out-of-work actor – was spoken to at length. Of course, Harrison denied any responsibility, and insisted that he was of good character. Others vouched for him, including fellow staff at *Halley & Meredith's*, who also provided an alibi, claiming to have shared a festive tipple with him once their work that Christmas Eve had finished. And indeed, when I was eventually shown a photograph of Harrison, it was a completely different man. This ended police enquiries at the store, for *Halley & Meredith's* had no other gentlemen employed in the role of Santa Claus."

"That can't have been the end of the matter?" someone else asked.

"Far from it." Grandpa Ludwig shifted to get comfortable in his armchair. "The news had got out, and there was wide concern in our town that someone – nobody knew who – had followed a child home and tried to force entry to his house. The police continued to ask questions for quite some time. It was perhaps two years later when my father finally contacted them to say that he was sorry for all this trouble, but that he felt I had simply fallen asleep while alone in the house on Christmas Eve and had suffered a nightmare."

"Did you?" my mum asked gently.

"Not a bit of it."

"So, what brought your father to this conclusion?"

Grandpa Ludwig shrugged. "It's anyone's guess, but it was quite a coincidence, I think, that around this time we learned the fate of Uncle Klaus. It seemed he'd been taken as a prisoner of war by the Soviets in 1944, and eventually, when hostilities were over, had been put on trial, accused of leading his unit in the massacres of civilians in Poland and Belarus. He was found guilty as charged and executed by hanging. I'm not sure of the exact date … but it was some time in December 1948."

Even my dad was speechless; evidently, he'd never heard this part of the story before either. The snapping and spitting of chestnut shells finally brought us round.

"Krampus," my auntie said with distaste. "What a horrible being to conjure up at Christmas time. The flipside of everything that is good and kind and forgiving."

Grandpa Ludwig nodded. "As Uncle Klaus said to me."

"When did he say that?" my dad asked. "If you never saw him again?"

Grandpa glanced up, his spectacles glinting with firelight. "Why … that final night before the war, after the argument with his twin brother, when he left our house in Mittenwald. At the time his exact words were lost on me, but since then I've remembered. He said: 'Be warned, Ludwig … there aren't just good fairies in your father's stories. There are bad ones too'."

THE TENTH LESSON

"Wonderful weather for it, eh?"

Tregarron smiled as he gazed out of the window at the umbrellas hurrying along Brewer Street, rain hammering them explosively. "Standard, isn't it?"

"Suppose so," Hadley sighed. "We all want snow, and nearly always get rain."

"We don't *all* want snow." Tregarron turned back to the table near the fire. "Have you ever considered how inconvenient that would actually be … if it snowed for real the way it snows in my books?"

Hadley chuckled. "There'd be some upsides. At least it'd stop my in-laws coming around for Christmas dinner."

Tregarron, who was tall, handsome and dark-haired for a guy in his late forties, resumed his seat. "You folk who actually celebrate Christmas don't half put up with some crap. And you fork out a fortune for the privilege."

Hadley – early fifties, heavy-set, with a mottled face and a mop of white hair – affected a more serious look as he tucked away his company credit card.

"Far be it from me to lecture one of our most successful authors," he said, "but if the general public ever found out what you *really* think about the festive season … i.e. that it's a massive con, it might spoil the illusion somewhat."

"They're all going home early," Tregarron replied airily. "They're too excited to pay any attention to our chit-chat."

On the face of it he was right. The pub was crowded to its tinsel-bedecked walls, but its hubbub was loud and good-natured, and no one was looking into this particular corner. Even the waitress who'd taken their empty plates had beamed after they'd paid, and skipped away, delighted with her generous tip.

"I wouldn't count on it, Adam," Hadley said. "You're 'Mr Christmas', remember?"

"They get what they pay for, Max."

There was no denying that either. Three hardback copies of Tregarron's most recent novel, *Wynter Fire*, lay on the table between them. Hadley had brought them so that the author could sign them as gifts for members of his family. But to call the new title a success would be the understatement of the year. It was only in its third month and already on its fourth reprint.

"The kids don't care what I think," Tregarron said, "and as for their mums and dads, well … if they don't already know that I'm selling a fantasy, there's something wrong with them."

"That splash in the *Telegraph* called you 'Christmas's biggest fan'."

"And?"

“And we estimate that we hit a sales spike of 75,000 extra copies on the basis of that feature alone. In one day.”

Tregarron considered. The double-page spread in the *Telegraph* had been Capricorn’s idea. In two successive years, he’d had phenomenal hits with Christmas novels for children. First had come *Wynter Frost*, which told the tale of a Victorian-era brother and sister, Sam and Evie Wynter, who got shipwrecked in the High Arctic, but were rescued from the ice by Santa’s elves and welcomed into the big man’s palace, only to be forced to earn their keep when Jack Frost brought an army of goblins to attack it. Second had come *Wynter Storm*, in which Sam and Evie led the elf resistance when a wicked interloper took Santa’s place and planned to send out broken and dangerous toys to all the children of the world. The latest adventure, *Wynter Fire*, which saw the intrepid youngsters head south for Christmas to try and reconnect with their families, only to find that it was now 1942, and that the Nazis had unleashed a winter monster called Perchta, had seemed likely to go the same way as the others, but to ensure it, his publishers had this time decided to make *him* part of the story. Learning that Tregarron had used the proceeds of the first two bestsellers to buy himself Wybrook Cottage, a lovely old farmhouse just outside Shere, in Surrey, Capricorn had suggested that, just for the duration of November and December, he turn it into a Yuletide shrine. They could then invite the press along to photograph it and interview him, so that he could spin a yarn about Christmas being the time of year he lived for. And so far, Tregarron had to admit, it had been very well worth it.

"It would help us all if we could maintain the pretence a little longer," Hadley added. "For the lifetime of the new contract at least?"

Tregarron nodded. He'd only recently signed a new deal to write three more Christmas books for Capricorn, a huge advance inevitably built into it given the astonishing profitability of the last three. "Don't worry. The secret's safe."

"What're you going to be doing, anyway?" Hadley asked.

"You mean over the next two days?" Tregarron shrugged. "Starting on *Sam and Evie 4*."

"Really?"

"You want it in the shops by next September, I'm going to need to deliver the first draft by March at the latest."

"No one said you have to work over …"

Tregarron grinned.

Hadley shook his head. "… the bank holiday."

"Relax." Tregarron finished his drink. "I'm kidding you. I'm actually off to the Caribbean. Not tomorrow, I hasten to add. Not on Christmas Day itself. That might be a bit of a give-away. I'm flying to Barbados on the 28th. Tomorrow? Well … I'm sure I can find some TV channel somewhere that isn't showing Christmas specials from twenty-five years ago."

"Good luck with that."

Tregarron shrugged his anorak on. "If nothing else, I can give my DVD of *Summer Holiday* some air-time."

"For someone who writes so lovingly about this time of year, you take my breath away."

"Sharon Penman."

Hadley frowned. "What?"

“She writes lovingly about the Middle Ages. But she’s probably glad she didn’t live then.” He headed for the door. “Happy New Year, Max …”

“And you, Adam.”

*

Tregarron huddled through the rain-swept Soho crowds, water dripping from the front of his hood. It always amazed him that Max Hadley, his editor at Capricorn Books, was baffled by his attitude. Why would anyone – any adult at least – think that Christmas was so wonderful?

It lasted one day in total, during which you invariably ate and drank too much and subsequently felt awful afterwards. You had to put up with irritating family members who normally you rarely saw. You spent money on gifts and cards for people you didn’t like. And in most cases, there was zero religious motivation. Virtually everyone Tregarron knew was an atheist or lapsed, yet they were giddy all December. How illogical was that?

He knew that the very few people aware he felt this way – mostly it was the editorial team at Capricorn – sniggered about it and called him ‘Humbug’. But Hell, Dickens himself had sold a dream of Christmas that wasn’t even close to being real. The great man had talked about good will to all men, about ‘God bless us, everyone!’, but that wasn’t replicated in real life. Most festive revellers were mainly interested in what was awaiting *them* under the Christmas tree. Meanwhile, old Charlie had even fooled everyone with his beautiful descriptions of a snow-clad London Town. Tregarron was sure he’d once read that Dickens had only seen a handful of white Christmases in his entire life. It was the same self-delusion now. Every shopfront glittered with fake evergreens adorned with artificial snow and imitation icicles, but out here in the real London, the sky was slate grey, the streets awash with rain. Not that this was stopping the commuters buzzing back and forth like eager children, bags bulging with parcels, eyes wide and bright. Each to their own, he decided, descending into Leicester Square Tube. Especially as after so many years in the writing wilderness, Christmas had become his meat and drink.

Normally at this time on a Thursday, the southbound stretch of the Northern Line would be empty once you passed Stockwell. Not today. With everyone knocking off early, it was standing room only as far south as Tooting Bec, and even when he reached South Wimbledon, plenty of the seats were still occupied. It was dark by now, of course, and as he walked across the car park to his Range Rover Vogue, felt slightly colder.

He drove west along Kingston Road, joining the A3 as it crossed Pyl Brook. By the time he reached the Tolworth Roundabout he'd given up all hope of finding a radio station that wasn't playing Bing Crosby or Kirsty McCall and The Pogues. But he was down in Surrey proper when he received the call on his hands-free.

It was from Sophie.

"You ringing up to do your annual impersonation of Scrooge's nephew?" he asked.

"I'm not inviting you to dinner tomorrow, if that's what's bothering you," his older sister replied.

"Good. Save us both a lot of embarrassment."

"It's just to say Happy Christmas. Surely you can't object to that?"

"Why not? I object to it every year."

"Adam, you really are an idiot."

"Really? Remind me, Sophie … which one of the two of us is a practising hedgewitch?"

"Can't you just be nice for once?"

"I *am* nice," he protested. "Talk to me about anything else, and I'll be nice as pie. Just don't talk to me about Christmas."

"You write about it all year round!"

"Yeah, like I used to write books full of sex and violence. To make money. Anyway, I don't know why a so-called Wiccan like you is bothered about Christmas. And please don't give me some crap about it being Celtic in origin. I've researched the subject far more than you and your crackpot crowd and I can assure you that the pagan thing is total bollocks. To start with, the festival of Christmas is *not* derived from Yule. Yule dates back to 400 AD at the earliest, whereas Christmas is referred to in Roman records some two centuries before that. Also, the birth of Jesus is *not* a Christianised version of the birth of Mithras … Mithras was not born of a human mother, and his cult came much later during the Empire. There is *no* provable connection between Christmas and the solstice celebrated by the druids. We don't even know if the druids celebrated the solstice because they didn't write anything down, whereas the Romans wrote an awful lot down about Christmas. Sorry to disappoint you, Soph, but Christmas is solidly Christian with a few pagan trappings that the Victorians added because they were midwinter emblems."

"Are you finished?" she asked patiently.

"There's more if you want it."

"Even if it's sacred to someone other than me, I can still respect it, can't I?"

"Yeah, and you can also recognise that I don't."

"I'm still going to say Happy Christmas to you, so there!"

"Fine, say it. Just don't be upset if I only respond with a Happy Hogmanay. At least the Scots can admit that their main winter festival is totally manufactured."

"Oh, you so need a lesson."

"Excuse me?"

"In manners if nothing else. In social etiquette."

"Perhaps I should get naked with you and your lady friends and dance around the woods when the moon's at its zenith, eh?"

"You know, Adam … pride comes before a fall. And the intellectually proud fall the farthest of all."

She hung up before he could reply, leaving him wondering if he'd gone too far. He and Sophie hadn't seen eye-to-eye for years, but perhaps there'd been no call for him to be so scornful.

The intellectually proud fall the farthest of all.

But was it really intellectual pride to be rational, to dismiss fairy stories and recognise when something was primarily a retail exercise? Good God, you could forget *A Christmas Carol*, you could forget *It's a Wonderful Life*. Without the shopping aspect, Christmas, like so many other religious feasts, would have shrunk to irrelevance long ago. Sophie didn't get that, essentially because she was a well-meaning but simple soul, who once, when she'd tried to explain her beliefs to him, had blithely confused Celtic mythology with Norse. It was no wonder he didn't take her seriously.

A *ping* from the dashboard drew his attention to the temperature gauge, which now blinked on and off. It only did this when it had dropped to two degrees and was anticipating icy roads. Tregarron was fascinated. It had been nine degrees at lunchtime. To his even greater surprise, dots of white began speckling his windscreen.

"Jesus!" he laughed.

It was snowing.

*

When Tregarron reached Wybrook Cottage, the snow was settling in inches rather than centimetres. He shifted his Range Rover into four-wheel drive as he slithered the last hundred yards along Packhorse Lane. When he reached his gateway, even he was transfixed by the dreamy sight that greeted him.

The seventeenth century property, built from stone but with a whitewashed exterior, black beams and a dome-like thatched roof, was already deeply blanketed, the slow heavy cascade of feather-sized flakes literally layering its millpond and extensive luxurious gardens. Spears of ice hung along its low-hanging eaves, warm lamplight glimmering out through the rind of frost that coated its mullioned windows. The generous tangle of fairy lights adorning the big hawthorn bush in the middle of the front lawn was also covered, but their ever-changing colours were still visible, and looked truly magical.

Actually, it was wondrous on *many* fronts. It had been snowing so hard here that the one vehicle on the drive, Ms Cale's Nissan Juke, was a rounded hummock of white, something Tregarron had barely seen in the UK. His dashboard barometer now read: – 5, which over the last couple of hours was a temperature drop of fourteen degrees.

The cold bit hard when he lowered his window to stick his key-fob out and auto-open the garage door.

Carefully, he crunched his Range Rover up the slight incline, slotting it undercover before applying the handbrake. Then he scrambled quickly out and around to the front door, which swung open to greet him. Ms Cale stood there. She was a no-nonsense widow in her fifties, slightly built, but very pretty, with long pale grey hair, which she habitually wore in a neat ponytail.

He stepped inside, brushing flakes off. "Wasn't expecting this."

"It's been like this for hours," she replied, closing the door.

"Hours? It was raining when I left London."

"Not here."

Tregarron shook his head at the schizophrenic nature of the British weather. His vague understanding was that it was ruled almost entirely by the moods of the Atlantic, which were utterly chaotic. So, yes, while mild winter weather was not uncommon, Britain, or parts of it, could still drop suddenly and unexpectedly into the deep freeze. He was distracted from this rumination when he entered the lounge, and standing to his left, found an oblong package, almost as tall as he was, wrapped in crisp red paper with silver bells all over it.

At first glance, it fitted with the lounge décor. As Capricorn had requested, the place was a shrine to Christmas: a berried holly wreath hanging on the brick hood over the blackened hearth, mistletoe dangling from the overhead beams, red linen and frosted pinecones on the coffee table. In the corner stood a real Christmas tree, adorned with toys and crackers and tasteful glass ornaments, and so large that it touched the ceiling. Thanks to the fat, ring-marked Advent candle held aloft by a three-foot plaster angel at the corner of the fireplace, all of this festive brocade now sat aglow in soft, warm light.

"Delivered today," Ms Cale said of the package. "A present, I supposed."

"A present?"

Tregarron might well sound surprised. The Christmas tree stood knee-deep in presents. Big ones too, all handsomely wrapped. But they were fakes, props provided by Capricorn. In reality, he hadn't sent anyone a Christmas present in years, and never received any in return. He attempted to move the item, but it was awkward, something heavy shifting inside.

"Any idea who delivered it?" he asked.

"None at all. I was shaking one of the mats outside around mid-afternoon, just after the snow started, and found it at the front step. I assumed the delivery driver had wanted to get back to the main road as quickly as possible. But no one rang the bell as far as I knew."

With some effort, Tregarron turned the object around.

"There's no label," Ms Cale said in her clipped, efficient fashion. "I've already checked."

"No shipping tag, either. Which is a bit odd."

He tore the wrapping off. Underneath, there was a blank cardboard box. Again, distinguishing marks were lacking. Thick tape was wrapped around it, but Ms Cale produced a pair of scissors and they sliced this away.

There was nothing initially startling about the object inside the box.

It was something you saw often in December. One of those nutcracker soldiers. Gaily painted, wearing a Napoleonic style red and green uniform, a shako on its head and a musket at its side, with bright blue eyes, a reddish protruding nose, flaring black moustaches, and a straight-line mouth composed of fierce white teeth framed by ruby-red lips.

No, there was nothing unusual about it. Apart from its size.

Because this one was six feet tall at least.

"Bless my soul!" It was a rare occasion when Ms Cale expressed amazement.

"It's just another decoration," Tregarron said, though he too was puzzled.

"An expensive one."

"Probably came from Capricorn and got delayed in the post."

This was certainly a possibility. When his publishers had first floated the idea that he deck his house for the season, he'd only agreed to it so long as *they* footed the bill. While it was Ms Cale who'd done most of the creative work, the decorations themselves – certainly the flashier ones – had been ferried over by courier, having been chosen and paid for by Capricorn themselves.

"Don't be too bowled over," he said. "You see these things in Costco. Bloody ridiculous really. I mean, seriously … who's got room for one of these in their house?

"Well, *you* have." Ms Cale moved in to take charge of it.

Tregarron went and draped his anorak on the hanger in the hall, and when he came back into the lounge, saw that she had arranged the soldier on the opposite side of the fireplace from the plaster angel. It stood with its back against the wall, like a sentry in a fairy tale.

"We should just bin it," he said. "You'll be dismantling all this while I'm away, anyway."

By prior arrangement, Ms Cale would come into the cottage while he was in the Caribbean and restore the place to its previous non-festive order.

"In the meantime, it's the final touch," she replied primly. "Your employers said that you might get another visit from the press over Christmas."

"Trust me …" he moved to the sideboard, where a decanter of fifteen-years-old Glenmorangie sat on a silver tray, "no one is going to interrupt their holiday to come all the way out here." He poured four fingers into a crystal tumbler and sipped deeply. "They especially won't want to come out in weather like this."

"On that subject, would it be all right if I finish now, Mr Tregarron? I know it's an hour earlier than usual, but I'm not sure how easily I'll get home as it is. I've prepared you a cold collation, so you don't have to worry about dinner."

She led the way into the dining room, where a small, neat spread awaited him: slabs of turkey and ham with dishes of onion-stuffing, cranberry sauce and mustard; a plate of spiced sausages and salad; some sliced tomatoes in garlic and pepper; and a hunk of Lancashire cheese.

"There're a couple of mince pies in the oven," Ms Cale added, "and the pouring-cream's in the fridge."

Despite the festive goodies, it looked so inviting that his stomach rumbled. "Wonderful."

"In that case, I'll clear up in the kitchen and head off."

Tregarron finished his drink and ambled upstairs to his bedroom, where he took a shower in the en suite. After that, tracksuited and wearing his slippers, he came back down and turned on the seventy-inch TV. Angela Lansbury appeared, weaving some ancient bit of Disneyesque sorcery to animate several suits of armour.

Briefly, he thought about Sophie. He shouldn't have been so rude to her. But the regret didn't last. Pouring two more fingers, he sat down and used the remote to channel-hop, supposing that he ought to be thankful to Christmas in one regard. It had been a hectic schedule recently, but at least there was nothing to get up for tomorrow morning.

"Does none of this affect you, Mr Tregarron?" Ms Cale asked. "Honestly?"

She'd come in from the kitchen wearing her waxed jacket and a heavy scarf.

"None of what?"

"Look at this place." She sounded wistful. "It's absolutely adorable. It's exactly the way a country cottage should be at Christmas time. And now with the snow as well …"

Tregarron snuggled back into his armchair. "I'm as much a lover of the seasons as the last tired suburbanite who sought solace in England's verdant heartland. This is how we are in winter. Come spring, summer … I'll expect my housekeeper to work similar wonders with my cottage interior."

She pulled her woollen gloves on. "I can't believe you're going to be on your own all day tomorrow. *And* on Boxing Day."

He shrugged. "A couple of days of solitude are well worth it when you consider that before the week's out, I'll be sailing the Caribbean."

Ms Cale tutted. "On your own."

"Shipboard romances happen, you know."

She tutted again, disapproving of what she considered to be flings. Her own husband had indulged in numerous of these during overseas business trips. That was why she'd divorced him. Tregarron was a singleton these days, but she still disapproved. Of course, she knew nothing about his own marriage, which had ended equally acrimoniously to her own but only after he and Emma had tried for about a decade to have children and finally, after two terrible miscarriages, had been forced to give up.

"Why don't you wander down to one of the village pubs tonight?" she suggested. "There are lots of ladies local to these parts who are very companionable. Well bred, well heeled …"

"And unfortunately past their prime. Just like me."

"Well, I'm sure you'll have a wonderful time on the ship." She headed into the hall. "I'll be off now."

"Enjoy the holiday, Margot," he said.

"Merry Christmas, Mr Tregarron."

When the front door opened, a freezing draft filled the downstairs, blowing the Advent candle out in the lounge. And then she was gone, the door closing again. Tregarron thumbed the button on the remote, but it was the same on every channel. If it wasn't Angela Lansbury, it was Julie Andrews, if it wasn't Alastair Sim grouching in black and white it was George C Scott barking in colour. However, before he found anything else, a key turned in the front door and Ms Cale came back in.

"I'm so sorry, Mr Tregarron." She stumbled red-cheeked to the lounge door. "It's my car. It's completely buried. I can't even get it out, never mind drive it home."

Glad to be away from such inane TV, Tregarron dug some trainers from the closet, along with a heavier coat than he'd worn earlier. Pulling up the hood, he accompanied her back outside. But it was true. The snow was astonishingly deep, not much short of a foot, and now, as a strong wind had risen, driving into them with raw intensity. They waded to the top of the drive. But as Ms Cale had said, her Juke was so comprehensively buried that it was scarcely recognisable as a vehicle. The garage was still open, so they went back in there to get shovels and spades. But though they got to work energetically, they barely made an impression, the flakes gushing down in torrents, the cold a searing blade.

"This is futile," Tregarron panted. "Come back inside." Indoors, he reclaimed his keys from his anorak. "The Range Rover's got four-wheel drive. I'll have you home in no time."

But Ms Cale looked shocked. "Mr Tregarron, in the short time I was with you, you drank at least five measures of whiskey."

"It'll be fine. The police aren't going to be stopping people in these conditions."

"Even if they aren't, they'll still be on road duty. They'll have to be. There'll be accidents everywhere. Suppose you have one? It won't necessarily even need to be your fault. They'll still breathalyse you. And what would happen then?"

He paused by the front door, already seeing the garish headline.

SPIRIT(S) OF THE SEASON!
Kids' Christmas author bladdered at steering wheel

'It wouldn't be a good look,' he admitted.

"Indeed not." She regarded him sternly.

It was an awkward moment. Tregarron obviously couldn't be blamed for these circumstances, but he couldn't help feeling as if he'd let her down a little. He didn’t consider that he had a problem, but he liked a drink, and perhaps he shouldn’t be too quick to dive into one whenever his working day was done. It was an old journalist’s habit, he supposed, one which during the final years of his marriage to Emma had only got worse.

“I don’t suppose a taxi will be able to reach us either?” Ms Cale said.

He pondered that. “Even if they did, they’d charge an arm and leg to run you the ten miles to Hascombe on Christmas Eve. Listen, you’re not going to your sister’s in Brighton until tomorrow morning. Is that correct?”

“That’s correct. I’m catching the mid-morning train.”

“So why don’t you stay here?” He shrugged. “We have rooms to spare, as you know. And I can drive you down to the coast myself, tomorrow. Like you said, I’ve nothing else to do.”

No doubt if, as a pillar of correctness, she’d been able to conceive of a solution other than spending the night under her unmarried employer’s roof, she’d have opted for that. But thanks to the unexpected blizzard, their choices were limited. They went upstairs together to decide which of the spare rooms was suitable, Tregarron glancing regretfully around the lounge first. He’d made the offer because he’d had to, but it wasn’t a joyous prospect, spending the night – even a night he had no fondness for – with someone who routinely behaved like a maiden-aunt. So wrapped up in these thoughts was he, that he didn’t notice the empty corner where the soldier had previously stood.

*

Ms Cale screamed.

Not only that, she dropped her plate, scattering cheese, meat and sausage all over the lounge carpet. Tregarron jumped in response, more consumables catapulting from his own dish. There'd been more than enough food prepared for them both and it was when they'd brought their suppers back into the lounge that Ms Cale had stopped dead, eyes locked on the Christmas tree, in fact focussed straight through it to another pair of eyes on the other side, a pair of painted blue eyes, which gazed out of the mesh of evergreen and tinsel with deep intensity.

"Good Lord!" She put a hand to her heart. "That gave me a turn."

"What on earth's the matter?" Tregarron asked, bending to scoop up his crumbs.

"I … well, I suppose if you didn't like him. I mean, it's your house. You can put him where you want."

"I'm sorry, what …?" His words stuttered out when he saw that the corner where they'd left the soldier earlier was empty.

"Over here." She pointed. "Behind the Christmas tree."

Tregarron was so stunned that more food slithered to the carpet. "I don't … I … you moved him over there?"

"*I* moved him?" Ms Cale said. "I presumed *you'd* moved him."

They approached together. The tall military doll was indeed standing behind the tree, but as he had been before: back straight, face forward, musket by his side. It was all the more remarkable because in only a foot or so of space, it would have been difficult for anyone to slot him in so neatly.

"You definitely didn't move him?" Tregarron asked.

"I struggled to get him into the corner. He's heavy."

Tregarron looked over his shoulder. "All the doors and windows are closed and locked, aren't they?"

They checked everywhere downstairs. But all entrances were shut. A hurried check upstairs brought the same result. When they came back down, they lugged the soldier out, its metal insides clunking and clanking, and examined it in detail.

"You've noticed it's got moving joints?" Ms Cale said. "Elbows, knees, wrists, fingers."

Tregarron *did* notice, and even though this was surely standard with these festive military figures, whatever size they were, it disconcerted him.

"You're surely not implying that it moved on its own?"

"I suppose …" she shook her head. "I mean … if it's a toy, a clockwork toy."

"That's ridiculous. They don't just start walking and go find themselves a hiding place. You're sure you didn't leave any doors or windows open during the day … even if only for a couple of minutes, while you were doing your chores?"

She paled. "You think someone might have come in earlier and be hiding?"

"I think that's more logical, don't you?"

They searched the house thoroughly, Tregarron armed with his old cricket bat, Ms Cale wielding the iron fire poker, which was purely an ornament, but would still pack a hefty whack. They checked under every bed, inside every cupboard and closet. They pulled the unfolding stair down and peered into the loft-space under the thatch.

There was no one in Wybrook Cottage but themselves.

When they went back downstairs, Tregarron was angry. His relaxed evening had been demolished, and he wasn't going to take it lying down.

"Out you go, my friend!" He grabbed the soldier round the neck and hauled it backward towards the hall door. "I'm pretty sure this is some kind of gimmick," he said. "And it's probably the work of my publishers. They've sent me a wind-up toy and it's gone haywire."

"Would they do that?"

"Normally they send me a bottle of malt. But perhaps they've decided I've got enough of those. Either way, it's going outside, where we won't have to worry about it."

Ms Cale opened the front door, and he dragged the effigy out, standing it upright just to the left of the entrance, facing across the drive onto Packhorse Lane. When he came back inside, he backheeled the door closed and went through into the lounge.

"It still seems odd," Ms Cale said from the hall. "What do we make of it?"

"I've told you what we make of it." He poured himself another four measures, which seemed reckless even by his own standards; he told himself that this time he deserved it, but he couldn't deny that, try to bury it under bravado as he may, he was also scared. "I'd ring Max Hadley right now and give him an earful, but I bet his phone's turned off."

"But if that really was just a joke by your publishers, they went to an awful lot of trouble."

"Someone did. Either way, the joke's on them. By morning it'll be so frozen they'll never get it working again."

Ms Cale pulled a curtain aside to glance out through the narrow window on the right of the front door. The soldier stood motionless, the entire front of its body, including its face, already plastered with snow.

Tregarron spent the next twenty minutes in the armchair, channel hopping again, angrily, sourly, drinking more whisky, incapable of ignoring the fact, no matter how hard he tried, that his explanation was ludicrous. Unable to stand the atmosphere, Ms Cale went through to the dining room, where she cleared the dishes away, taking everything to the kitchen. The remaining food she wrapped and stored in the fridge, the crockery and cutlery she put in the washer. She spied the scrunched-up mass of cardboard and Christmas paper that the soldier had come wrapped in. She'd tied it with string and left it by the back door, intending to throw it out when she returned here in a few days. But now seemed as good a time as any.

Picking the bundle up, she unlocked the back door and stepped out into the narrow passage between the rear of the house and one of its closed-up outbuildings. It was filled with snow to a depth of maybe ten inches, which on any other night she would have considered remarkable for southern England. At the front of the house, the gate to the passage was closed, but at the back, a left-turn led into the extensive rear garden, where the wheelie-bins were kept.

She plodded slowly down there, her smoky breath whirling in the wind. The whole process took her no more than a couple of minutes, but even then, before she re-entered the house, she stopped in her tracks, staring dumbly down the passage towards the front.

Where the gate now stood open.

She glanced at the back door. She'd wedged it to prevent the wind closing it behind her. The fact that it now stood wide open could also have been down to the wind. But she doubted it, especially as, looking back along the passage, she saw fresh dints in the snow.

Footprints.

She hurried inside, where fragments of white led across the kitchen into the scullery, the door to which stood open. The light was off in there, but there was sufficient from the kitchen to reveal that it was empty, but also that the door on the far side of it was also open.

"Mr Tregarron!" she yelled. "Come quickly!"

It said a lot about his own state of mind that he was at her shoulder in a shot.

She pointed to the door at the back of the scullery. It was a door they rarely used, and which dated to the cottage's former existence as a working farm. It had once connected to the old servants' quarters, a section of the house that was only accessible from here, but in recent decades the whole place had been modernised, so now it connected with the entire upper floor.

Cursing, Tregarron swung around, dashing through the dining room and the lounge, into the hall. Yanking the front door open, he stared out. The soldier was gone. He raced back through the house, and when he reappeared alongside Ms Cale, had the iron poker in his fist.

"This has gone far enough," he growled.

"Look." She pointed at a kitchen drawer, which hung open, spilling cutlery and other bric-a-brac.

"It's a burglar then," he said. "An everyday thief. That bloody thing must be a case or suit. There's an actual man inside it."

"Wait." She put a hand on his arm. "Don't go up there angry. It still may just be a joke."

"A joke! Someone walking around my house uninvited?"

He yanked his arm loose and ran at the back-stair.

*

Tregarron came to an abrupt halt at the top, eyes scanning the darkened passage ahead, along which several bedroom doors stood open, each one shedding even darker darkness.

"I'm warning you," he shouted, hefting the poker. "Don't make the mistake of thinking that just because I write children's books, I'm some kind of sissy."

There was no response.

He advanced a few yards, eyeing the carpet. But if there'd been any snow left on the intruder's boots by the time he'd arrived up here, there was no trace of it now.

"Look, if this is just a joke … if you work for someone who thinks he's found something out about my real attitude to Christmas, maybe I can live with that. Maybe there won't be any need for rough stuff. But you've got to step out where I can see you."

In direct response to this, he heard a sudden *whirring* and *clicking*, as if gears and wheels had gone into motion, and a steady repeated creak: the sound of timber under pressure.

And then it appeared, at the far end of the passage, from a bedroom on the right.

The soldier.

Initially he saw it only in profile. Until it swung about to face him.

Tregarron insisted to himself again that it was someone inside a suit. And yet the inflexibility of its painted grinning face, the jerkiness of its movements, the ramrod stiffness of its posture made this seem incredibly unlikely. Abruptly, the soldier went *en garde*, tilting sharply forward, musket levelled at waist-height. To Tregarron's even greater incredulity, he now saw a glint of steel at the weapon's tip.

With slow, heavy steps, and a further creaking of its lifeless limbs, it advanced. It had closed a quarter of the distance when he saw that string and tape had been used to fix in place the so-called Kitchen Devil, the sharpest knife in the drawer, as an improvised bayonet.

Tregarron turned and ran, blundering straight into Ms Cale, whom he hadn't realised had come up behind him. The two of them fell in a tangle, she gasping, he swearing. And still it came, the landing juddering beneath its feet. Already, it was less than ten yards away, steel lowered for the fatal lunge.

Tregarron yanked his housekeeper up by the collar of her sweater, throwing her through the nearest open door and diving through it after her, hitting the light switch en route. It was the fourth spare bedroom, currently being used for lumber. He slammed the door behind him and grabbed for the nearest packing-case. It was heavy and filled with junk, but he dragged it forward and rammed it against the door, before stepping back, sparkling with sweat.

Ms Cale jumped up alongside him, whiter-faced than he'd ever seen her, visibly shaking.

Beyond the door, the creaking and *whirring* ceased. But they could sense the presence on the other side. The door shuddered to a heavy blow. Another followed and another. Then several inches of the Kitchen Devil came through. It briefly stuck there, only to be waggled from side to side and wrenched back out of sight. A second passed before it pierced the door again. And again, and again, each time Ms Cale letting out a terrified yelp. Tregarron turned to the shelves behind him, snatching more odds and ends, throwing them into the box in an effort to increase its weight. Further blows struck the door, the blade punching clean through.

"For God's sake, stop!" Ms Cale shrieked.

An even heavier impact landed, this time in the very middle of the door. This one wasn't delivered by blade, but by blunt instrument. And they soon realised why. Because that whole section of central panel, weakened by puncture marks, was now the target. Inevitably, when a second hefty impact landed, it was smashed clean through – by a clenched wooden fist.

"All right, enough's enough!" Tregarron bellowed. "Whoever you are, you've got us scared, you've got us confined. The house is yours, you can grab whatever you want. But don't waste this opportunity. I've got my mobile with me …" this was a lie, of course but the intruder didn't necessarily know that, "and I've already called the police. These weather conditions are hard, but armed burglars on the premises will still bring law enforcement running. I estimate that you've got three or four minutes at the most."

Silence followed. A pondering silence this time, as if Tregarron's words had hit home. Then, abruptly, there was more *whirring* and *clicking*, and a further creaking of timber and clumping of feet, but this time the sounds diminished as the intruder manoeuvred away from the bedroom door.

Tregarron glanced at Ms Cale, intrigued. The feet started down the staircase.

"It's worked," he whispered.

Ms Cale looked hopeful but put a cautionary hand on his arm.

There was fleeting silence as the intruder reached the ground floor, but then they heard the backdoor slamming shut. Tregarron leaned one-handed against the wall. "Well … it was a novel way to break and enter." He sounded relieved. "Could only bloody work at this time of year, of course."

They waited a little longer, until the silence downstairs was ear-pummelling.

He straightened up. "*We've* got to get out of here too."

Ms Cale looked frightened again.

"We can't do nothing," he said. "This is a serious crime and we have to report it."

"You mean leave the house?"

"We can call the police right now, but it's anyone's guess how long they'll take to respond in this weather. And if they don't arrive soon, he might come back."

"But how do we manage it?"

"The Range Rover. How else?"

"But you've been drinking."

"We're running for our lives, Ms Cale. I think that might cover us."

She contemplated this, before tiredly nodding.

They moved the packing-case aside and listened again at the door. Nothing stirred. Ms Cale stepped back as Tregarron took the handle. He held his breath, and yanked it open. The corridor was clear. He looked in both directions, still seeing no-one.

They scurried out, heading not towards the back-stair, but towards the main staircase, which descended into the hall. They scrutinised this from the top before even commencing a descent. Again, nothing moved down below: the front door was closed, the carpet illuminated by the Christmas lights shining out from the lounge. Tregarron held his breath as he went down, Ms Cale following on catlike feet a few treads behind.

They stopped close to the bottom, glancing along the hall in both directions.

Left, they could see all the way into the lounge. Again, nothing moved. Right, the door stood open to Tregarron's office and darkness lay beyond it. That was potential danger, but they were only a couple of yards from the front door, and Tregarron now hurried forward, his housekeeper close behind. When he turned the catch, the door opened easily; in fact, it blew open, flakes gusting noisily through. But stealth didn't matter anymore. Already, they were outside, struggling through shin-deep snow to the still-open garage.

Thanking God that his keys were still in his tracksuit pocket, Tregarron opened the Range Rover's driver door and scrambled in behind the wheel. As soon as Ms Cale had climbed into the passenger seat, he brought the big beast to life, knocking it into reverse.

And immediately encountered difficulties.

Despite its four-wheel drive, it hit the deep snow heavily, sluggishly. There was minimal traction in its tyres, and he had problems steering.

"Damn it to bloody hell!" he swore, fighting to control the car, which was moving every which way as it descended the drive.

With a clunk, it struck the side of Ms Cale's Juke.

"Mr Tregarron!" she protested.

"I'm sorry … "

He looked out through the windows, but they were obscured by flakes. His wipers thudded back and forth to little effect, though from those few glimpses they afforded of the outside, he discerned that he'd now turned partway around as if he was on a pivot – so that his front end was pointed onto the garden.

"*What the bloody hell's going on?*" He applied the handbrake and climbed out.

"Mr Tregarron!"

Once he was outside, though inundated by flakes, he spotted the problem straight away.

The Range Rover's tyres were punctured and flat, shredded in fact, hanging in ribbons.

His mouth dropped open.

"*Mr Tregarron!*" Ms Cale screamed. It wasn't a protest now; it was a warning.

He spun around, and just in time, as the lurching, clunking figure approached fast across the lawn, still with bayonet extended.

Tregarron rushed for the driver's door, only for the wind to slam it in front of him. He yanked it open. The wind pushed it back again. Frantic, he caught it, slid his body around and fell into his seat – and only just in time. The bayonet struck the door and sliced clean through, the blade emerging through the upholstery. Tregarron might have been skewered had he not kicked his door back open. There was a *crack*, which they heard even over the sound of the blizzard. The steel remained embedded in the door, so it could only be the musket.

Tregarron pulled the door closed, hit the ignition and tromped the gas. Still in reverse, the Range Rover grated along the flank of the Juke, before he threw it back into first and then second, flinging his wheel to the right, attempting a three-point turn. He repeated the manoeuvre twice before the figure of the soldier came directly into his headlights.

Tregarron punched his foot to the metal.

The powerful car all but jumped the five yards between them, the collision massive, the target sent hurtling backward, crashing high into the hawthorn clump. Fleetingly, a curtain of billowing snow screened it, before it cleared again and they saw the stiff twisted shape slipping downward through the branches, bringing wreathes of fairy lights with it.

Seconds passed as they sat listening to the hiss of snowflakes on bodywork.

"My God," Miss Cale whispered. "If that was a man in a costume … what have we done?"

Tregarron didn't bother replying that he was long past believing the costume theory. Or that by now he didn't care either way. But he knew that they had to check. He opened his buckled door and climbed out, attempting to loosen the knife, though it proved to be jammed fast. Ms Cale came around the vehicle to stand alongside him. More flakes swept them as they ventured onto the garden. An only vaguely distinguishable figure lay just ahead, half in and half out of the hawthorn, tangled in flickering fairy lights.

Up close, it had taken a severe beating, its limbs askew, its paintwork scarred, a huge, brutal gash in the centre of its body.

"He's good and dead," Tregarron said matter-of-factly.

"There's nothing good about death, Mr Tregarron." Ms Cale advanced.

Tregarron didn't accompany her. Nor did he feel chastened by her comment. The probability was that he'd witnessed too many grisly death scenes during his journalist days to feel anything like empathy. On which subject, Ms Cale now knelt down alongside the prone shape, even leaning over it.

"Errr, Ms Cale," he said, "you're a little close …"

"He may be badly hurt," she admonished him.

But he wasn't.

As the right hand rising towards her attested.

Ms Cale didn't see that, or the broken strand of fairy lights it was clutching.

Tregarron only saw it when it suddenly sparked.

When actual contact was made, it was quite spectacular, a glaring flash of blue light, the woman jerking and juddering in silhouette.

With a BANG, the property plunged into total blackness.

Tregarron bolted for the front door, throwing himself through it, intending to bar the horror outside, but the door wouldn't close, swinging back at him. He tried it a second time, with the same result. Only to remember that he'd unfastened the catch. He scrabbled with it in the darkness, the snow lashing his face, blinding him. Though he could see just enough to realise that a charred black form, *whirring* and *clicking*, was now lumbering towards him.

He tore himself away, running into the lounge. Where he stopped rigid, looking around.

Whrrr ... click ... creeeaaak ...

The sounds changed timbre as they came inside the house.

Tregarron spun frantically.

It would search in every obvious place. It would have all night to search.

Frantic, he threw himself to the ground and scrambled on all fours towards the Christmas tree. As hollow feet clumped towards the lounge door, he pushed the fake presents aside and insinuated himself amongst them, pulling them in behind him, all but wrapping his body around the base of the tree so that its toy-laden boughs covered him from above.

It came in.

Stopping in the middle of the room.

Tregarron's sweat turned to ice as frigid air blew through the house. He hardly even dared breathe, though it seemed insane. Could it actually hear, this lifeless, creaking automaton? Could it see, this thing made of timber? Was there a reasoning intellect in that clockwork brain? How was any of this possible? What devilry had created it?

And then something astonishing occurred to him, a possible explanation that at one time would have been too ridiculous to contemplate. Even as he lay hunched under the Christmas tree, his mouth slackened open. It couldn't be. It just couldn't …

With another creak, the thing moved. Tregarron went stiff, terror clawing his insides as it thudded across the carpet. But it didn't come in his direction. Instead, it went through into the dining room, blundering against the sideboard, ornaments and decorations falling and breaking. The hubbub continued as it moved on into the kitchen, Tregarron still listening. He gazed out between the parcels stacked in front of him, eyes now adjusting to the gloom – and a tiny point of green light materialised on the carpet only a foot or so away. With a jolt, he realised that it was his mobile phone. In the desperate back-and-forth of the last few hours, it had been knocked from wherever he'd left it.

Tregarron watched it closely as he listened to the sound of the intruder's feet thumping up the back-stair. It wouldn't be up there for long of course, not when it couldn't locate him. As stealthily as possible, he shifted parcels aside, reached out and gripped the phone. Mouth close to its facia, he speed-dialled one number in particular.

He'd no idea what time it now was, but nor did he care.

The voice that answered did so with a quick, terse 'Hello?' and sounded wary. And well it might. Sophie had first been thrown out of the family home when she was nineteen, their mother having reacted furiously to her declaration that she was forsaking Christianity for paganism. "I'm not having witchcraft in my house!" the feisty old lady had shrieked. "There'll be no devilry under this roof."

Devilry.

"What the hell, Sophie!" he hissed, wanting to shout but not daring. "Are you responsible for this insanity?"

"Oh, I see …" Her tone altered, became lofty. "Is it possible that you've changed your tune?"

"My tune?" He was incredulous.

"Learned your lesson?"

"Are you serious? How in the name of God did you make this happen?"

"It isn't difficult when you know how."

He was amazed at how casual she was being.

"A few of us got together," she said, "made an incantation …"

"I can't believe you've done this!"

"Done what? Made you appreciate the season a little more?"

"Stop talking like a lunatic! This thing's deadly! It's already killed my housekeeper!"

"Ms Cale is dead, is she?" She sounded amused, though not because she thought it was funny, more because she was humouring him. "Really?"

"Yes, *really*! You silly bitch!"

"Adam, what're you talking about?" Her voice tautened. "Ms Cale's dead? Seriously?"

"Yes, seriously … you think I'd joke about that?"

"How is that possible?"

"She was electrocuted!"

"Oh … oh my God." Briefly, Sophie sounded lost for words. A genuine note of fear had crept into her voice. "You're sure she's dead. I mean, she's definitely …"

"No, I'm not *sure*. But it hardly bloody matters, does it! At this rate, *I'll* be dead too!"

"Where are you?" she asked.

"Tucked up in a corner of the house, trying to …"

"Stay where you are. I'm coming over."

"You won't be able to get through the snow, you idiot!"

"Just stay where you are."

"Sophie!"

"Look, I'll call this thing off, but it'll take a little time. It'll be much easier if I'm actually there." And before he could object again, she'd hung up,

"*God damn it!*"

Only then, belatedly, did he realise that he wasn't whispering anymore? In fact, that he'd been shouting at the top of his voice.

His ears strained, expecting the sound of feet on the back-stair. But now, even more eerily, there was no sound at all. He lay rigid, wringing with sweat. That same terrible choice faced him: stealthy retreat or wild flight? Not that there was anywhere to fly to, except out into the blizzard, where he might perish by other means.

But anything was better than staying here.

Quietly but quickly, he pushed the parcels aside, slithered out and got to his feet.

And promptly, a strand of fused fairy lights was looped over his head and pulled tight. Tregarron gagged as hard wooden hands twisted it at the nape of his neck, as it cut deep into his windpipe. He choked and kicked out and cast around for anything that might help him. His hand touched the Advent candle. It was hefty, but it was only made from wax. Then he remembered the angel that held it.

The three-foot plaster angel.

With a strength he'd never known he possessed, literally the strength of the demented, Tregarron jerked his whole body sideways, causing his assailant to totter along with him. The noose loosened, and he thrust his fingers underneath it, forcing it open and dragging it backward over his head. Free, he grabbed the angel, the strength of the insane again aiding him as he swung it around in a great heavy arc, smashing it into the soldier's head with a force so explosive that it jarred his shoulders and shattered the angel into millions of pieces.

The soldier's head was torn clean off, the pulverised lump of wood hurtling across the lounge, bouncing from the brick fireplace like a football.

Tregarron backed off, gasping, goggling in disbelief at the headless figure now *whirring* madly as it cavorted in the dimness, its arms flailing, only bits of broken timber where the neck had been, the stem of its metal spine jutting up from the hollow, wheels *clicking* and turning in the recess beneath.

He didn't wait to see more but charged into the lounge and out through the front door, galloping down the drive regardless that he might trip or slip, and turning right along Packhorse Lane. He didn't know how long he ran for, a mile maybe, taking country roads at random, hoping they'd shortcut him to the nearest major route before his energy began to flag. He was crossing a narrow bridge over the River Tillingbourne when his stride inevitably started shortening, his feet stumbling, his breaths turning to steamy sobs.

Exhausted, shocked, stressed beyond imagining, he found himself tottering to the wall of the bridge. Leaning on it, wheezing, he used the flat of his hand to wipe the flakes from his eyes. Ten feet below, a sheet of thick ice covered the river surface, inches of snow laying over it in a crisp, smooth mantle. Lovely, gorgeous, the perfect winter scene. But what was it he'd said to Max Hadley only a few hours ago?

Have you ever considered how inconvenient that would actually be ... if it snowed for real the way it snows in my books?

Good Lord, how prophetic. Because though he was running now from something he felt certain would kill him, it was fast dawning on Tregarron how numb his extremities were, how hard his heart was beating just to keep the blood flowing through his frigid limbs, how much it hurt his chest just to suck in this deep-frozen air. And how far he still had to go before he was likely to find shelter of any sort …

"Adam?" came a concerned voice.

He glanced up and saw that a Jimny SUV had arrived on the bridge from the other direction and was now parked only a few yards away. He recognised it as belonging to Sophie before she even got out and came hurriedly over, her tousled blonde hair packed under a parka's fur-rimmed hood.

"Oh my God," she said slowly, her lovely face written with genuine concern. She grabbed his hands. "You're freezing."

"Yeah?" He'd have laughed but his teeth were chattering too much. "There's a b-bloody surprise."

"You've come out in this wearing a tracksuit and training shoes?"

"Sorry … didn't have much time to get my winter woollies on."

She shook her head. "I'm the one who should be sorry. I had no idea this would happen. Don't worry. I've stopped it now. It'll take a little time, but it's already coming to an end."

He nodded dumbly. He might have berated her more had he not been so cold.

"We need to get back to your house, Adam," she said pointedly. "I need to check on Ms Cale."

Ever the nurse, he thought.

It would baffle people that his sister, as well as being a practising hedgewitch had also been an NHS nurse for the last thirty years. But apparently, or so she'd told him, it was more common than people realised. While he was thinking this, she led him to the car, assisting him into the front passenger seat, fixing his seatbelt, and going around to the driver's side.

"I'm so sorry about this, Adam," she said as she drove them back towards Wybrook Cottage. Her Jimny, which also had four-wheel drive, had no problem in the snow, though it proceeded jerkily. "It seemed a harmless enough idea. I thought you might actually enjoy it."

"Enjoy it?" It was this incredible statement that finally snapped him from his reverie. His voice turned harsh. "*Enjoy it!* Dear God, Sophie! I don't know what world you and the rest of your midnight hags dwell in, but I struggle to see how anyone could find *this* enjoyable!"

"No one was supposed to get killed."

This time he did laugh. Loudly and scornfully. He was still laughing when she eased the car up onto the drive, just behind his Range Rover, which sat skew-whiff.

"My God," she breathed.

"Considering you don't believe in that guy, you call on him an awful lot."

"Where is she?"

He pointed across the lawn, to where an inert form still lay amid blackened snow and a bundle of shorted-out fairy lights.

Sophie powered her window down to look properly. Outside, for the first time in what seemed like hours, the groan of the wind was lessening, the cascade of flakes ebbing.

"If this spell of yours takes time to reverse itself," Tregarron said, "we should wait in the car. He may still be lurking around."

Sophie turned her head to look at him. "*Who* may still be lurking around?"

"Who else are we talking about? The soldier."

She looked bewildered. "Soldier?"

"Why are you just repeating everything I'm saying?"

"Because you're not making any sense."

"For Christ's sake … what exactly is it that you think you've done to me tonight?"

She shrugged. "Invoked a localised winter storm. To give you a white Christmas. Doesn't go very far. Just a few miles in each direction, Wybrook Cottage at the epicentre."

Tregarron stared dumbly at her. "Winter storm? You didn't do anything else?"

"Was that not enough? Most people would give their left arm for heavy snow on …"

“Just get us out of here!” he interrupted. “Right now! Right bloody now!”

Sophie said nothing but continued to regard him with a confused expression.

“Sophie!” he yelled. “For God’s sake!” He grabbed her shoulder and shook her. “Look, I’ll explain on the …”

Her head lolled sideways.

Behind it, the yellow handle of a screwdriver jutted from the back of her neck. One of his own screwdrivers, he realised dully. One of those he kept in the garage.

His eyes roved upward.

The soldier was standing outside the car. Its head had been restored, though it wasn’t a pretty sight, the paintwork scarred, the face splintered, the heavy screws that had been driven into its neck sitting at crazy angles.

Screaming, Tregarron leaned over his dead sister to hit the ignition, but the soldier was quicker, reaching through the open window and snatching the keys first. Still screaming, Tregarron threw himself back against the passenger door, knocking it open, falling out.

It came around the Jimny as he got to his feet. It was completely unstable now: lurching, seesawing, turning parts visible through the rents in its wooden flesh.

Tregarron left the drive, stumbling into the cottage’s north garden, but he was bone-weary, his chest aching abominably, his thoughts spinning. There was nowhere left to run even if he had the strength for it. Instead, he turned and tottered through the snow-buried stalks of a flowerbed, veering towards a great white mound close to the rhododendron hedge bordering the property. The soldier followed, slower than before but relentless. When Tregarron got to the mound, he fumbled along the top of it, hands too numb to feel the chill, fingers scrabbling over stacked logs – and then closing on the solid hickory shaft of the wood-axe he'd been seeking.

He wrenched it from the snow and spun around. The figure was already so close that he couldn't take a proper swing at it. So, he backed off again, onto flatter, more even ground.

Still it followed.

"I get it now, I really do," Tregarron panted. "Because there's only one explanation, isn't there? Whoever you are, you came here to punish me … for rejecting and at the same time exploiting the magic of this season." Still it followed him, still he stumbled backward, the axe hefted at his shoulder. "And maybe that's only right. After all, they call Christmas Eve service the Nine Lessons and Carols. But now, maybe, just maybe … *I have a lesson for you!*"

His final words were a roar as he came to a halt, swinging the axe up, over and down, burying its steel head in his enemy's timber shako, splitting it clean through the middle, along with the wooden skull beneath.

The soldier's head, patched up already, fell in two halves.

"You see, the thing about Christmas … it's for *children*!" Tregarron swung the axe again, cleaving the soldier's left arm at the shoulder. Springs and cogs fell out. "It's all about *children*!" He struck again, scything into the side of its neck, a brutal fissure zigzagging down the centre of its chest. "So, if I can't have children … why should I have Christmas?" With the fourth blow, steel met steel as the axe bit into its innards. "Answer that and I'll spare you. But you can't, can you?" The fifth blow struck its right shoulder; that whole arm was lopped away. "No one can! Ever! Never

ever!" The sixth blow found the neck again, and what remained of the head was sundered from its torso for the second time that evening.

This time with an air of permanence.

The mangled figure sagged where it stood, knees buckling, clockwork guts disgorging as it broke open all the way down the middle.

Tregarron managed to strike it one more time before it hit the ground, a butchered, shattered hulk. It twitched for a few seconds, very feebly, its *clicking* and *whirring* gradually slowing until at last they stopped altogether, and the mechanism lay still.

Tregarron stood over it for several seconds, too weary to think straight. Too weary even to hold the axe, the handle of which slid through his sweat-damp palms and clattered down. He nudged at the fallen shape with his toe.

"You know the irony of it," he told no one in particular. "You came here to punish me. But all you've really done is help perpetuate this thing you despise … because, gosh darn it, you've only gone and given me my next book."

He tried to laugh, but he couldn't, of course, because in truth it wasn't that funny.

Exhausted and aching, he made to walk away. And heard a long, low creak.

He stared back, alarmed. But the smashed effigy lay motionless. Puzzled, he glanced further afield, but all he could see was the dark hulk of the house against the December stars, which were now clear, the storm having completely abated. He looked left and saw the rhododendrons. Then behind and in front of him, and finally down at the flat, white surface under his feet.

The millpond, he realised. He was right in the middle of it.

That creak?

He listened again but heard only a steady dripping sound. From all around him.

I've stopped it now, Sophie had said of the fleecy maelstrom she'd conjured. *It'll take a little time, but it's already coming to an end.*

Tregarron breathed out, but no longer saw his breath.

The creak sounded again, torturous, extending away on all sides.

The millpond's edge was a good forty yards away.

Tregarron went for it.

But the ice gave way on twenty.

THE STAIN

The problem with British horror cinema is that it peaked before it should have done. Chillers like 'The Curse Of Frankenstein', 'Peeping Tom' and 'The Haunting' are deservedly among the most lauded horror movies ever made, but they are congregated around the end of the 1950s and the beginning of the 1960s, which now, in movie terms, seems an age ago. Purists, of course, would argue that this is no bad thing. British horror movies of that era broke a number of important taboos, which otherwise would have continued to hamper the makers of fantastic films possibly for decades to come. While Hollywood was still safely fighting giant bugs in the black and white deserts of the atomic age, in Britain blood ran a vivid shade of red, women had become sexually aware, and the horrors of the disintegrating mind proved far more chilling than any number of little green men armed with death-rays. Unfortunately, this cutting-edge approach was as misunderstood then as it often is now, usually by the movie makers themselves. Enough, it seemed, was never as good as a feast. Each outing had to be more disturbing and more terrifying than the last, which was soon proving difficult with increasingly educated and sophisticated audiences. The emphasis thus shifted to causing shock rather than creating fear, to amazing cinema goers with gaudy displays of ever worsening depravity rather than leaving them frightened to turn out the light. And, of course, once it began, this vicious cycle could not be broken, mainly because it was quick and simple to produce, but above all because it was cheap. Studio execs called for ever more gore, ever more nudity, ever more explicit violence. At length, by the dawn of the next decade, British horror cinema was little more than an outlet for crude sexual sadism, and had shed every scrap of its artistic heritage.

Perhaps the most glaring example of this freefall into self-indulgent bad taste was Lonnie Abelard's 1969 thriller, 'Daemonia'. Launched amid a blaze of alleged bizarre phenomena, this supposedly ground-breaking investigation into the evils of modern day Satanism hit new lows of mind-numbing carnage, and featured such degrading and repulsive spectacles as faeces-eating, projectile vomiting, ritual disembowelment, cannibalism, necrophilia, overt blasphemy and an anal rape performed by a monstrous demon equipped (though thankfully we were spared a visualisation of this) with a gigantic, spike-tipped phallus. Never had the viewing public witnessed such an uncontrolled extravaganza of carnal brutality. Never had movie watchdogs been as scandalised. Not surprisingly in that age of immature rebelliousness, 'Daemonia' was a box office smash, though thankfully its merits, or lack of them, have been re-assessed since. To this date, it remains banned in many countries.

John Jackson-Brown
Understanding Extreme Cinema, 1982

*

As he drove out of London that Friday morning, Rick was despondent, a feeling compounded by the fact that it was only ten days to Christmas.

He knew that, by rights, he should now be relaxed and looking forward to the season ahead. But that was impossible. While everyone else he knew was winding down their workload, planning shopping trips and sticking up decorations, he still had this forthcoming weekend to deal with. And even though the weekend itself should have been an exciting prospect – a no-name writer like him being linked for all eternity with the legendary Lionheart Productions, not to mention a horror movie that had now become a cult favourite – it wasn't.

His spirits didn't lift even when he got out of the log-jammed traffic of the city and into the countryside. The weather wasn't helping. It was bitterly cold, and as he cruised west on the M40, the normally verdant Home Counties lay bleak and leafless under skeletal trees and patches of frozen snow. This was the way it should be, of course, in mid-December, but an icy easterly wind and a lead-grey sky threatened much worse to come. It would be bad enough having to spend a whole weekend away from home with people who irritated him but being marooned for several days longer than that because of foul weather would be close to unendurable.

Rick got his foot down hard.

The things you had to do to make a living.

*

It never ceased to amaze Rick how drab and uninspiring Pinewood Studios could be.

Considering this was the epicentre of the British film industry and the home base for innumerable Hollywood blockbusters, he'd never once been here and seen even a Z-list star, let alone anyone approaching the dizzying majesty of a Johnny Depp or Angelina Jolie (both of whom, to name but two, had reputedly been on site when he was present once before). To tell the truth, he'd hardly ever seen anyone of significance. The car parks were always chocka, and invariably there were security guards around; normally these were burly ex-paratrooper types, who'd stand with their arms folded, glaring at you as if they were absolutely certain you shouldn't be there. But generally, given the size of the complex, it was startlingly quiet, both indoors and out. He'd lost count of the number of lengthy, oak-panelled corridors he'd strolled along, spotting endless famous names emblazoned on office doors but never hearing a noise from the other side or seeing anyone going in or out. He usually ran into a technician or two: technicians were as numerous at Pinewood as security guards, but then they were numerous on industrial estates too, and on factory car parks, and in the basement areas of office blocks. There was nothing in particular about dour-faced men slouching around in paint-stained overalls and low-slung tool-belts that reminded Rick he'd suddenly arrived at the throbbing heart of moviedom.

Being honest, he didn't feel like he'd done that at all. Not even when he saw Stafford Wilkes standing outside the front door of the main building, chomping as ever on a fat King Edward cigar. In appearance terms, the one-time powerbroker of British film had changed little. Okay, he was paunchier than he had been in his pomp, and whiter and thinner on top, but he was still tall, still tanned, and he still had a penchant for sharp pin-striped suits. The one he currently wore was an elegant three-piecer, its double-breasted jacket buttoned up smartly. His black leather shoes glinted like mirrors, despite the slush he was standing in. By contrast, Rick – in jeans, trainers and a hooded, grey sweatshirt – looked like some disreputable oik from the wrong side of the tracks. But the great man wouldn't bat an eyelid about that. These days, he couldn't afford to.

"Rick!" Wilkes shouted, as he sighted the battered blue Allegro coming up the slip-lane. He waved a big brown hand, then grabbed up a bulging holdall.

Rick slowed to a halt and parked. As he did, the doors to the main building opened and a young woman came out. It was Tanya, Wilkes' fourth wife and possibly the hottest yet. She was only short – five-three at the most – but with soft, shoulder-length blonde hair and an extraordinarily pretty face. At present she wore a heavy waxed jacket, with a pink tracksuit underneath, and white ankle warmers above her sneakers. The unflattering ensemble all but buried her usually pert figure. She tended to look better in the efficient, charcoal-black skirt suits that she reserved for business meetings: these were often tight to the point of being severe, but they showed her curves to perfection. They also hinted accurately at her true personality. Tanya Fielding (she'd determinedly stuck with her maiden name), might be Stafford Wilkes' youngest wife to date, but she was by far the canniest. Her cute 'little girl' looks were a perfect mask for the calculating mind underneath.

She too was carrying a holdall, alongside a briefcase, and she seemed pleased to see Rick. She hurried daintily down the steps as her husband eased himself into the back seat.

"Everything all right?" Wilkes asked in his gravelly trans-Atlantic voice.

"Great," Rick replied. "You guys ready then?"

"Absolutely."

"This is really good of you, Rick," Tanya said, climbing in beside her husband. "You sure you don't mind driving?"

"No problem."

"It's a long run."

"Hey look …" Rick tried to feign willing. "If we've gotta go, we've gotta go."

He glanced into the rear-view mirror, and for a moment it struck him how surreal the whole thing was. Stafford Wilkes, the onetime mogul of British cinema, admittedly retired for the last few years, but now bouncing back … in a beaten-up K-reg Allegro.

In former decades, the great fellow wouldn't have gone anywhere without his stretch-limo; if Rick remembered rightly, Wilkes had been one of the first people in Britain to own such an extravagant vehicle. Even in the light of the financial disasters he'd suffered since, it was hard to believe that Lionheart Productions' newly re-appointed managing director (not to mention his wife, who, despite being only thirty, was now the company's executive producer), would lower himself to this. It illustrated more than words ever could just how far 'Papa Bear', as he'd been known at the height of his career, had fallen.

"Roni, Graham and Gail are making their own way down," Tanya said, interrupting Rick's thoughts. "Roni and Graham live in Wimbledon, so it's probably for the best, and Gail's been with her mother all week in Southampton, so it's even easier for her."

"Fine," Rick replied. "Everyone in?"

They grunted in the affirmative, so he swung the car round in a three-point turn and drove back towards the main gates. He tried not to think too much about the three people Tanya had just mentioned, but it was difficult to discount them from his miserable ruminations.

Roni Maplewood, Tanya's so-called 'Head of Production', was even younger than Tanya – twenty-three at the most – and less than a month ago she'd been a trainee script editor on one of the lower rated TV soaps. Lacking everything but ambition, she'd eventually been shown the door on that show, but prepared to exchange a decent salary for a title, she'd now made the superficially impressive leap into the movies. Graham Grundy, Tanya's PA, was another incredibly young and inexperienced chap, who again seemed bereft of any real qualifications. Rick didn't like to speculate what Graham's true purpose was in Tanya's life, though to be fair the guy was at least affable, whereas Roni affected a bullish assertiveness, presumably to make up for her lack of talent. That left only Gail Withers, who of the three was by far Rick's favourite. An unpretentious secretary, Gail had no highfalutin notions about what she did for a living, and was always happy to make idle chit-chat with him when the others were too busy to come to the phone and explain why he still hadn't been paid for his latest bit of work.

It was almost tragic that Wilkes himself, who was now past seventy, his wife – who, for all her habitual name-dropping, was still a newcomer to the industry –

and these three untried nonentities constituted the entire staff of the once mythical Lionheart Productions. Eight months earlier, when Rick's agent had phoned him to ask if he'd be interested in scripting for the famed movie house, he'd hit the ceiling with excitement. That evening, he'd taken Shirley and the kids out and treated them to champagne at the local *brasserie*. Only over the following weeks, during a series of progressively less thrilling meetings, had it become clear to him that, by 2005, Lionheart was only a threadbare shadow of the unstoppable force, which, back in the halcyon days of the '60s and '70s, had stood alongside Hammer and Amicus as a keystone of modern British horror, and whose crowning glory had undoubtedly been that lurid gothic romp, *Daemonia*.

"You know, Rick, we're all going to get rich off this deal," Wilkes assured him.

"I believe you, Stafford," Rick replied, not bothering to add that he'd be glad just to get a decent wage for a change.

"We appreciate you sticking with us, Rick," Tanya added. "It's been a hard road, but we like your writing, and we're going to make it worth your while."

"I'm looking forward to it," Rick responded, refusing to buy into the bullshit and now concentrating on driving. "Everyone warm enough?"

They replied that they were, though he noticed that Tanya still hadn't taken her waxed jacket off. The heating was working, but the Allegro was so old that there was a permanent dankness to its interior. With three of them packed inside, this would soon transform into a discomforting humidity. It was going to be a long journey down to the New Forest, he realised. And if the weather worsened – which it did, because by the time they reached the north Hampshire border, fresh snow was falling – their progress would be slow.

*

Rick Schaefer had been a full-time author for six years now, but he was already cynical about the whole business.

He'd first entered the writing world in 1988 as a trainee newspaper reporter, and rose steadily through the ranks until 1996, when he made the position of Features Editor for one of the dailies. It was good money and easy work for a writer of his ability. But it wasn't a great challenge. In response, he started to pen fiction, and at length, while still employed by his newspaper (but mainly because of the job he'd *first* held on leaving school), he secured a trial script for *City in Flames*, the popular TV soap opera about fire-fighters. The script was good enough to draw him to the attention of the programme's senior staff, and a succession of commissions subsequently followed. Soon, he'd sold options on a couple of his own original screenplays as well and was starting to pick up payments for short story sales, which tended mainly to be horror. By the time he was thirty-four he was earning enough from his freelance writing to consider dumping his day job, and any doubts about this that he and Shirley might have had were put to bed two years later when Rick's newspaper announced a forthcoming round of redundancies, and in the first instance was seeking volunteers. Rick had no hesitation in stepping forward. It meant that he'd receive a decent pay-out, with which he could underwrite his first year as a freelance, and even if the worst came to the worst, the kids were now old enough for Shirley to go back to work, so they'd still have a regular income. In the first couple of years it worked better than either of them could have hoped, the cash piling in. Then, unexpectedly, the soap work, Rick's bread and butter, hit a brick wall. As happens so regularly in the world of television, a new and aggressive series producer had been appointed to the show, and his first priority was to expunge all traces of his predecessor. Rick, who was only ever employed by the programme on an episode-to-episode basis, was one of the easier ones to dispense with.

Embittered but unperturbed, he ploughed resolutely on. Short story sales were still mounting, though without the back-up of a TV deal, the remuneration for these was so meagre that it was difficult to justify continuing to write them. On the advice of his agent, who thought he could put his horror skills to more profitable use, he began to write speculative movie scripts instead. Although none were sold, they were polished enough pieces of work for his agent to advertise him to a different market. This was how he'd come to the attention of Lionheart Productions, who, after years of inactivity, had recently re-launched under their original founder, Stafford Wilkes, and planned to make a new slate of low-budget horror movies, cashing in on renewed interest in the genre following the success of *The Sixth Sense* and *The Blair Witch Project*. At the time, of course, when he'd first had this mentioned to him, Rick hadn't realised that the whole thing was being funded on a shoestring, and was mainly for the benefit of Wilkes' ambitious young wife, while Wilkes himself intended to stay largely retired. Eight penniless months down the line, however, and the writer was no longer under any illusions. Not only that, the experience had soured him to the point where Shirley said he'd undergone a personality change.

Rick was now a colder, grumpier individual, who took nothing at face-value. Despite everything he'd endured, he always tried to remain civil with his fellow professionals, though it was increasingly difficult for him to feign enthusiasm for all but the most promising-sounding projects. He hadn't yet voiced it, but as far as he was concerned, this weekend was the final throw of the dice for him and Lionheart. He'd only agreed to come at all because Wilkes himself had telephoned and asked if he would. They'd changed their plans, the grand old man of British film had said. They were going to shelve all the new ideas they'd been playing unsuccessfully around with, and were re-visiting *Daemonia*, Lionheart's whopping hit of 1969. They were going to feed off its success all over again.

Rick had asked what Wilkes meant. Were they going to remake the film?

Wilkes had replied gravely: "No. There's no possibility we can remake *Daemonia* to anything like the same professional standards that we did in '69. We don't have the money or the facilities anymore. Neither could we recapture the mood or moment. That was the late-60s. It was a raunchy, sleazy era, when anything went. The Devil was getting hip, but God was still respected enough for audiences to want Him to win. The time was perfect to adapt Willis Roxborough's book."

(Willis Roxborough was the young Oxford don who, back in the 1920s, had written the novel *Daemonia*, though his version had been a strait-laced black magic thriller in the establishment-friendly style of Dennis Wheatley. Naturally, come the late-60s, Wilkes had given it a far more fiendish treatment.)

"So, if we're not going to remake it, Stafford," Rick had asked warily, "what *are* we going to do? Make a sequel?"

"Something like that. I want you to come and join me, Tanya and the rest of the team at Godley Grange for a weekend."

"Godley Grange?"

"You know, where we filmed the original movie."

"I remember it, sure. But when?"

"Next week?"

"I see. Next week."

If Rick had sounded unhappy on the phone, that was because he was. By this stage, he was at his wits' end with Lionheart Productions. He'd wasted time, energy, and most criminally of all, *ideas* on them. He wasn't in the mood to be jerked around. But the fact that it was Wilkes who'd made this call, rather than Tanya, had added a touch of respectability to it. In addition, there'd been the not inconsiderable factor of *Daemonia*, one of horror's great hits.

Rick wasn't at all sure what this mysterious invitation signified, but his interest had been pricked just sufficiently for him to trust Lionheart one last time. So here he was, chauffeuring his employers into the wintry depths of the New Forest. It had stopped snowing about an hour before, but a thick groundcover remained. Inside the forest, this was reduced to perhaps a couple of centimetres, and was largely invisible thanks to one of those foggy glooms so typical of December afternoons.

"Well, a desolate environment like this seems very appropriate for the mood we hope to create," Wilkes mumbled through his cigar smoke.

"There's no doubting that," Rick replied, though *he* was talking more about the mood that Lionheart had created for him personally.

"Ah," Tanya said. "We're here."

"To their left, two tall brick gateposts came into view. The ornate wooden gates between them stood open, revealing a churned snowy track that wound quickly away into a denser, tree-filled darkness.

"Good," Tanya added. "It's open. The others must've arrived already."

Rick said nothing but turned onto the track. A couple of minutes later, they came in sight of the bridge. Godley Grange, though not located on an island as such, was separated from the sparse network of single-lane roads that ran back and forth through the New Forest by a cut-off from the River Lymington, which flowed along a deep gully all the way to the Solent. As such, the house was only accessible by car if one drove over an infamously narrow and rickety-looking bridge. From this point, Rick proceeded with extreme care. The timber structure, which – incredibly, but perhaps unsurprisingly in modern, bureaucracy-riddled Britain – could not be replaced with a sturdier modern version because it was subject to a preservation order, rumbled and shook as the car crawled across it. In the glow of the headlights, its aged planks glistened under a coat of frost, and, as there was only a flimsy guardrail to either side, the slightest loss of control could have sent them plummeting.

Thankfully it was only twenty yards to the other side, and they were soon on the woodland drive again and at last grinding to a halt on a wide, pebbled parking area in front of Godley Grange itself. Night had now fallen properly, and little of the country house was actually visible. Rick remembered it from the original movie as a big, imposing palatial residence, a Victorian gothic in the truest sense: built from dark stone, but consisting largely of towers and turrets, with brief sections of flat, balustraded roof between them, and reams of carved ornamentation on its upper facades, including gargoyles, griffins and eagles. At present, however, it was just an immense black outline with stark shafts of electric light slanting out through its ecclesiastically arched windows.

Light also shone brightly from the open front door, where a female shape stood waiting, arms folded against the chill. From her lustrous copper-red locks, Rick recognised her as Roni Maplewood.

"So, we've got the scary castle," Wilkes said jovially, not yet having spotted his wife's Head of Production. "Now all we need is a monster."

Rick didn't say anything.

*

Inside, Godley Grange had been furbished for the modern age. Old world items remained in the way of antiques, framed portraits and traditional rural décor, but generally speaking its interior was twenty-first century.

Its downstairs contained a central hall, in the middle of which a grand staircase rose to the first floor. To either side of this there were large but comfortable reception rooms, one adapted into a lounge, the other into an ornate dining area. In addition, there was a kitchen, two sculleries, and a reading room/conservatory. Upstairs apparently (because they hadn't yet checked), there were twelve sizeable bedrooms, six of which had been made up for them by the housekeeper. She, incidentally, had now left for the evening. There wasn't a twenty-four-hour staff presence at Godley Grange, and Rick couldn't help wondering the reason for that: was it too expensive a luxury, or were none forthcoming to take up the job?

The lounge, which was spacious, was ready to receive them. Its massive hearth was stocked with wood and burning cheerfully. There were easy chairs to either side of it, two facing sofas, and in front of those, a low central coffee table on which a pile of papers was already scattered. Roni, it seemed, was hard at work, or at least that was the impression she was hoping to give.

"Mr Turner's not here yet," she said, as they removed their coats. Roni took Tanya's for her. "But he rang through. He got held up. Said he'd be about an hour late."

Tanya nodded, half-smiled in that enigmatic way of hers and made no verbal reply, which irritated Rick to some tune. No-one had said anything to him about their not being the only ones here this weekend; he certainly didn't know any 'Mr Turner' and couldn't guess who he might be or what role he had to play, so wouldn't it at least have been polite of her to explain?

Roni was still talking. "Gail's in the kitchen, making herself useful. I told her to get a pot of coffee on. Should be ready by now. We've only been here twenty minutes, ourselves."

"It's nice and warm," Wilkes said, rubbing his hands together.

"It's like this all over the house," Roni replied. "Must be well insulated."

"We haven't heard any bumps in the night yet," came a voice from the other side of the room.

This was Graham. He'd been seated by a bookcase and leafing through a couple of dusty old volumes, but now he came forward smiling. He was tall, fair-haired and trim, casually but always fashionably dressed – on this occasion in stonewashed denims – and improbably handsome, rather like one of those male models whose angelic faces and immaculate hairstyles adorn the walls of salons.

"Only because there are fewer young ladies here than usual to faint dead away at the sight of you, darling," came Tanya's chirpy reply.

It always fascinated Rick how the woman behaved with Graham, compared to the way she interacted with the others. The young guy seemed to have less to do than anyone at Lionheart, yet Tanya, who affected a demeanour of tolerant coolness with her other full-time underlings, laughed at his jokes, including the bad ones, and even exchanged cheeky quips with him. Of course, this didn't mean there was anything going on between them. And, in truth, there probably wasn't, because why would she risk muddying the waters with her husband when there was still so much benefit to be drawn from staying married to him? But it spoke volumes about Tanya's immature man-management skills. Yet again, Rick felt convinced that Lionheart Productions would fail to regain its former status so long as Tanya Fielding controlled even one percent of its operation.

If her husband had any doubts, however, he wasn't showing them at present. "Let's take a look around," he said keenly. "It's thirty-five years since I checked this place out. Come on, we can find our bedrooms later."

Despite the long, cramped journey they'd just made, Wilkes' trademark pinstripe suit was as pristine as ever. The knot of his blue silk tie wasn't a millimetre out of place. Briefly, the firelight shone on his big, broad grin, and for all his seventy-plus years he was still a tall, wide-shouldered fellow, every inch the Papa Bear of movie making legend. Fleetingly Rick's confidence was restored.

Their first port of call was the immense, stone-flagged kitchen, which though it contained a hob, and a huge, cast-iron range smelling strongly of oil, was essentially new. Gail Withers was in there, and now provided them with mugs of steaming coffee. Compared to Roni, who, with her flowing red tresses, stylish clothes and full-on make up, was always glamorous, Gail was rather plain looking, but still attractive in a cheerful 'girl next door' sort of way. She was slim but shapely, and currently dressed in a t-shirt, jeans and white plimsolls. Her long dark hair was tied at the back in a bun.

Rick smiled as she handed him his mug. She returned the smile.

"You presumably heard about the problems we had while we were actually making *Daemonia*?" Wilkes asked as they stood there and sipped.

Rick nodded. "Who hasn't?"

"And it doesn't trouble you at all?"

Rick shrugged. "If you mean will it worry me to spend a couple of nights here, then no." He didn't add that he was less concerned about spending a weekend in Godley Grange than he was about how long it would be before he actually hooked up with an outfit that wasn't just *playing* at making movies.

Wilkes began to poke around in the large kitchen. One door he opened connected with a cellar stair that dropped steeply into darkness. He fumbled inside it, found a switch and turned on an electric light. Without further ado, he went down into the subterranean section of the house. Rick followed him and found – rather to his amusement – that all the others were also trooping obediently in pursuit, like a set of lapdogs.

The cellars consisted of several low arched chambers, all made from dank brick, with narrow dingy passageways connecting them. They were stacked with boxes, lumber and ancient pieces of broken, cobweb-covered furniture. Rick was interested to spot a dog-eared paperback copy of the novel, *Daemonia*, lying on a cluttered shelf. Almost certainly, it had been left over from the original shoot. In fact, by the looks of it – because it was thick with dust – no-one had picked it up since. He flicked through it, seeing pages yellow and loose in their binding. The cover was so marked with mildew that it was difficult to make out the illustration; he could just about identify a grotesque, idol-like head complete with glaring ruby eyes.

"Now then," Wilkes said from the main chamber, "this is just as it was back in '69."

Rick went through to join him. The others followed, only Gail halting to glance at the paperback.

"I mean, there's more junk in here than there was," Wilkes added – he was standing in the midst of a large, barrel-vaulted room that was again crammed with the wreckage of former furnishings – "but the dimensions of the place haven't changed one bit. Anyone remember? We shot a particularly controversial scene in here."

Rick remembered it well. Early on in the movie, one of the secondary characters, though she'd been played by a leading actress to lull the audience into a false sense of security – much the way Janet Leigh was used by Hitchcock in *Psycho* – was dragged down here having been tied up in a burlap sack. The cellar had been clear of rubbish at the time, and its floor painted with a pentangle surrounded by astrological symbols. The sacked victim had been thrown into the middle of this, then beaten to death with clubs by a gang of hooded Satanists. That beating had gone on for nearly a full minute, the victim writhing and giving muffled screams, and all the time her blood soaking through the sacking in blossom-like patches. As Rick recalled, that particular scene had either been trimmed to the bone or cut completely from the version of the film that had finally made it onto TV in the 1990s.

"Oh yes," Wilkes confirmed, sounding delighted, "this area hasn't changed at all."

Rick glanced down at the floor. It was covered with rags, fragments of paper and even old, desiccated leaves. He kicked this debris aside and imagined he could see the faded remnant of a pentangle point painted on the cement.

"So, what do you think?" Wilkes asked him.

Rick glanced up. "Excuse me?"

"Do you believe the production was cursed?"

Rick shrugged. "It was definitely a troubled shoot, Stafford. I've heard about that. But, if you want the truth, I always assumed that was just the publicity machine going into overdrive. I mean, which horror movie worth its salt didn't have strange problems during production? It happened with *The Wicker Man* and *The Omen*."

"But *Daemonia* was made before any of those."

"Okay, you had the idea first. Well done."

"The point is," Tanya put in, "Lionheart's experiences were genuine."

"I see." Rick decided not to ask how Tanya Fielding, who hadn't even been born in 1969, could possibly know anything about it.

Wilkes took up the story. "We had star walkouts, power failures, unexplained accidents on set. We even received threats from a local devil cult."

"But that was the reason you chose to film down here in the New Forest, wasn't it?" Rick said. "This area's always been known for witchcraft activity."

Wilkes appeared not to have heard him. He led them back upstairs, continuing with his recitations. "Of course, it didn't stop there. The writer-director, Lonnie Abelard, never worked properly again. I mean *Daemonia*, when it was released, was a sensation, a massive hit. It should have made his career. But he died soon afterwards, in relative obscurity."

As Rick had heard it, Lonnie Abelard, though undoubtedly a talent – it was his vision that had turned *Daemonia* from a pot-boiler into a major event – had also been a drug addict and had owed money to the underworld. Not long after making the film, he took a sideways step into what was then the quick-earning and fashionable realm of soft porn. If his mob and drug involvements hadn't killed his career, *that* surely would have.

"Our own problems were well documented after *Daemonia* was released," Wilkes added as they re-entered the kitchen. "As a company we went into a slow but steady decline."

"But Lionheart continued making films into the early '80s, didn't they?" Rick said. "And two or three of them were quite successful."

"Yes, but behind the scenes a lot of things were going wrong for us."

Probably due to financial mismanagement, Rick thought, which wasn't at all unique to the film industry and very rarely needed a supernatural explanation. From here on, though, he decided to cease playing the devil's advocate. Like it or not, he was relying on these people to make him a bit of money, so it wouldn't do just to be negative for the sake of it.

"The final proof is Godley Grange itself," Wilkes said. "It's allegedly been haunted ever since the shoot wrapped."

"I've heard about that," Rick had to admit. "Didn't the owner sell up and move?"

"He did," Tanya said. "And the next owner didn't last very long either."

"Who owns the place now?" Rick asked.

"An Aussie millionaire," she replied. "But he's only hung onto it for as long as he has because he doesn't live here. He leases it to holidaymakers, which explains how *we* got hold of it for the weekend."

"And the haunting's still supposed to go on?"

"That's what we're here to find out." Wilkes grinned, clapping Rick on the shoulder. "Not only that, if there really *is* something bad here, we're not just going to find it … we're going to bottle it and sell it."

*

"We're going to make a movie about the original movie that was *Daemonia*," Wilkes said across the dining table.

"A movie about a movie?" Rick replied uncertainly.

This odd notion had taken him more by surprise than it normally would have as he was still struggling to get his head around the surreal scene back in the lounge, where Roni, Graham and Gail were kneeling at the coffee table, trying to get spirit writing from a planchette and pen. Thus far they'd had no results, but if their collective qualifications for contacting the dead were as unimpressive as they were for working on movies, it was hardly surprising.

"That's right," Wilkes said. "It'll concern itself with a fictional attempt to re-make the film here, in this very same house. Only, whereas the first-time round we received warnings of impending disaster, this time all Hell is going to let loose."

Rick stared across the lamp-lit table at Wilkes and Tanya. A heap of disordered paperwork was now spread between them. Tanya had put a fetching pair of glasses on. Wilkes had even taken his jacket off. The atmosphere was all business-like, though Rick still wasn't sure he'd heard the pitch correctly.

"Let me get this straight," he said, "we're going to make a movie about an attempt to re-make the original movie?"

Wilkes grinned. "Is that sexy or what?"

Had anyone else, especially Tanya, made this pitch to Rick, he wouldn't have been able to avoid scoffing, but as it was Stafford Wilkes it had to be given further consideration, and gradually he began to see how the idea could work. Okay, at first it sounded scatty, but when you looked at it from a hard, money-making perspective, it made a certain kind of sense. It would allow you to draw on all the garish, glorious and highly expensive elements of the first film without actually having to recreate them. It would enable you to tell a completely original horror story but at the same time bask in the blood-red glow of a pre-existing one that already had a brand name and a cult following. There was an aesthetic factor too. Doing it this way, you wouldn't just be re-making a tried and tested hit, or knocking off a cheap sequel that was exactly the same as the first outing, you'd be continuing the story, adding to it, but at the same time taking it off in a new and surprising direction. As far as Rick knew, this particular strategy had never been tried before.

Wilkes continued. "Most important of all, we're planning to go straight to DVD with it. It'll be released as part of a two-disc boxset. The second disc will be the original movie."

That too made sense. Cinematic release always gave a movie greater kudos, but the costs of even limited distribution could often be prohibitive, whereas licensing the property straight to DVD was relatively inexpensive and would bring in your first batch of profits straight away. Rick felt the idea growing on him, though Tanya clearly saw a need to explain further.

"*Daemonia* has never been released on DVD in the UK," she said. "It was released in the States, but that was a poor-quality print and it only had a short run before it was deleted. This time, though, we're going to use a letterbox print, digitally re-mastered so we've got vivid colours and a crystal-clear picture. It'll also be fully restored – every single piece the censors cut out will be back in its rightful place. Plus, there'll be lots of extras, documentaries and such. We reckon that, on its own, this would be a huge seller, especially if we go big on the supernatural occurrences that resulted. But add this second movie to the mix – a further chapter in the *Daemonia* story, as made by the original company, filmed on the very same location, and with lots more scary publicity wrapped around it – and we reckon we'll make a fortune."

Rick turned to Wilkes. "You still own the rights to *Daemonia*?"

"I've re-acquired them from Universal."

"So, all we need now," Tanya chipped in, "is a script for the new movie."

Rick nodded sagely. "Which you're going to have to pay the full whack for." He gave her a frank stare. "No more mate rates, Tanya. If you guys can afford to buy the property back from Hollywood, you can certainly afford to give me a fifteen-grand advance on a two percent principal photography fee."

"Don't worry about that," Wilkes said.

"But I *am* worried about it, Stafford. I'm skint, and in debt up to my eyes."

And suddenly it all began to pour uncontrollably out, probably because of the self-confident glow radiating from his hosts. How many of these seedling movie projects he'd been attached to, how much work they'd demanded, and yet how few of them had actually translated themselves into payments of any respectable size.

"Shirley's tired of being the sole breadwinner," he complained. "And she's sick of glib reassurances from me that everything'll be okay, which even *I'm* now stopping believing. I mean, where's the money I need to live actually going to come from? Half the time you folks won't return my agent's calls. You don't return mine unless it's something *you* want to talk about. Of the few cheques I've had, several have bounced because you accidentally forgot to sign them. We've had silly games over contract minutiae, which have dragged on for months, and all that time I'm not earning. Christ, I've just driven us from Pinewood and I've not even had anyone offer to share the cost of petrol …"

"Point taken," Wilkes said, looking embarrassed and not a little surprised.

"Rick," Tanya hastily added, "I assure you you'll be recompensed for everything you've done for us. In full. No question of it. But don't you think this idea's got legs?"

Rick sighed. No matter how forcefully or emotionally he tried to get into it, Tanya's one great skill was avoiding conversations about money. There was never, ever any way to draw her on the subject. "Yes," he said, wearily but truthfully. "Yes, I do."

She smiled. "Then let's thrash out a storyline this weekend. While we're actually here, soaking up the ambience of the place, going over the strange events that happened on this very spot … then you can take it all back home to Edgware on Monday, and write us a startling script."

"Only if there's a startling cheque in my pocket."

"No problem," Wilkes said gravely. "You've been mistreated up to now. We've taken advantage of your good nature. But that won't happen anymore, my word on it. Now that we've finally got a workable idea, we want to get cracking."

Rick nodded. It wasn't the first time he'd heard this sort of thing from them, but they had to start the ball rolling somewhere. "How do you want to approach it?"

Tanya began shuffling papers. "I reckon the first way to deal with this is for us to understand what the actual problems were that afflicted the original production … to learn exactly what it was about the first movie that had such devastating consequences for so many of those involved. That way we'll have a real solid basis for our horror."

Rick nodded again.

She went on. "I've watched the original film several times now and studied the script. Of course, I don't know anything about devil worship or any of that stuff …"

Or movie making, Rick thought to himself.

"… but it occurred to me that there are two very graphic Black Mass scenes in the film, and maybe some of the incantations used for them, incantations which I believe were lifted directly from Roxborough's book, might have been the real thing."

Rick eyed her. "You're saying that staging those Black Mass scenes might actually have caused a demon to be raised?"

"Well, I wouldn't put it in such blunt terms as that. But it could have invited, shall we say, some sort of malediction."

"It's a start-point, I suppose."

"Yeah, but unfortunately it doesn't work," she said. "As I say, I wasn't sure about it, so I sent a copy of the script to an acquaintance of mine who's a member of the Church of Satan. He studied it too, then came back and told me the whole thing was a load of bunk. It sounds as though Willis Roxborough was making it up as he went along. None of the rituals or incantations used in the book, or subsequently the film, was even close to being authentic."

"And this Church of Satan guy is reliable?" Wilkes asked.

She nodded. "The next thing that occurred to me was … maybe the cause of the trouble was something more abstract. Perhaps it was simply the nature of the film. You know what I mean; this has happened before … where a movie is so evil, so wicked, that it can't be made without causing these weird kinds of reverberations."

"But the film wasn't evil, was it," Rick argued. "Look, it was a good movie, Stafford, but no offence, its main shock factor came from it being full of tits, bums and lashings of obviously fake blood. It was a farrago of horror clichés and late-60s raunch. It wouldn't disturb a five-year-old today."

Wilkes regarded him coolly and blew out a long stream of cigar smoke. "Remind me never to give you an attachment to our publicity department."

"All I'm saying is that it's highly unlikely a film like *Daemonia* would invoke paranormal chaos."

Tanya took her glasses off at this, seemingly irritated. Clearly this was the inspired and astonishingly original tack that she'd been hoping to take with the movie, and Rick had scuttled it at the first turn. However, before she could say anything, there came a thunderously loud knocking at the front door.

They glanced at each other uncertainly, and then Roni stuck her head in. She'd arrived at the dining room so speedily that a cynic might conclude she'd been waiting just outside, earwigging. "I'm guessing that'll be Mr Turner," she said.

"Good," Wilkes replied, rising to his feet. "Now perhaps we can get somewhere."

*

Mr Turner – Wallace Turner, to use his full name – was apparently a medium, and the moment he came into the house he struck Rick as the complete caricature: he was a tall but painfully thin man of indeterminate age, with a shock of untidy snow-white hair and a thick, floppy moustache of the same colour. Beneath his coat, his clothing consisted of a worn, flower-patterned sweater, patched at its elbows with leather, a pair of shabby green corduroy trousers, and working boots that were badly scuffed around the toes. His eyes were tinged an unhealthy yellow and seemed to dart from side to side as if everywhere he looked, he expected to behold some ghastly vision.

He didn't waste time with introductions. After a very brief conversation, during which he dumped his haversack (because he too, it seemed, had been booked for the weekend) and greeted everyone with surprisingly firm handshakes, he strode forward into the hall, and paused, a haggard expression immediately imprinted on his face. Once again, those tortured eyes swivelled in their sockets.

"This house is definitely active," he said. "I sense an unhealthy influence resident here."

"Anywhere in particular?" Tanya asked.

"Not actually here, in this hallway, at this moment," Turner replied. "But it lurks somewhere inside this building. It's listening to us right now."

"Is it confined to any specific area?"

"No. It has free rein. But only within these walls."

Roni and Graham exchanged discomforted looks, which almost made Rick laugh out loud – they actually *believed* it. Not that he himself was a total sceptic, but he'd now had a chance to look the place over and, okay, it was a big, isolated mansion surrounded by dreary woods, but there was no atmosphere here; at least, none that he'd noticed.

"Can you tell us more about it?" Wilkes wondered. "This thing?"

"It hails from ..." Turner broke off to nervously lick his lips, "it hails from one of the lower regions of the spirit realm."

"What does it look like?" Tanya asked.

"I don't know. I'm not sure I *want* to know."

Turner strode on, and the rest followed. A tour of the house should be his priority before anything else, he said. He needed to get a feel for the place.

The reading room/conservatory was the ideal spot in which to spend a balmy summer evening. Now, however, only a couple of pieces of cane furniture occupied it, while its tiled floor, which covered a considerable expanse, was scattered with fragments of withered leaves. Doubtless it would normally be filled with exotic plants, and in July and August the French windows would be open and the ornate fans that hung overhead revolving lazily. At the moment it was cold and bare. Beyond its glazed panels, an extensive portion of lawn sparkled under moon-lit snow, but was overhung by masses of drooping, skeletal branches. There was no electric light in here, only an ethereal glow shining in from the outside.

Tanya turned to Turner "Anything?"

Turner shook his head. "Nothing in here. This room is an add-on, of course, a sort of annexe." He addressed Wilkes. "Was it part of the building when you were originally filming here?"

"Yes," Wilkes replied. "Though I think it's been renovated and modernised since. It was a lot more Victorian then, all scroll ironwork. We used it as a hothouse, filled it with jungle flora. There was a nasty scene in here, when one of our heroes was killed and hidden under the foliage, and afterwards Venus flytrap-type plants grew out of his body and vampirised anyone who came close."

Rick didn't bother to comment that this incident had featured some of the worst trick-photography in the film. As he recalled, though, the general impact of that scene had been effective; it was a new and novel idea that plants could also be demonically possessed.

After the conservatory, they wandered into the dining room. Tanya's paperwork was strewn across one end of the table, but otherwise the place was undisturbed. Solemn faces gazed down from a row of ancient oil paintings. The panelling in there was polished teak.

"This room's relatively clean too," Turner said, walking around the table. "I sense some residual energy here, which might actually pre-date the time when you filmed."

"The house was first built in the 1840s, as I understand it," Wilkes remarked, "so it could easily have picked up one or two ghosts of its own."

Turner pursed his lips. "There's nothing especially malignant, but I sense unease. If other spirit persons inhabit this place, they're not content. There is something in this building that's extremely hostile. To them, to us, to everyone and everything."

For the first time now, Rick noticed that Tanya was taping the conversation. For some reason, this aggravated him: it was so typical of her. She was always so efficient, so competent, so capable of running a small company like Lionheart Productions undoubtedly was these days, and yet key things – like knowing one end of a script from the other – eluded her. During the course of their relatively brief (but, at times, seemingly torturously long) involvement, Tanya had given Rick her views on how a film script should really be written, often quoting verbatim and at length from film writing books that he himself had read years before. The fact that the only thing she really seemed to know was what she *didn't* want, and thus repeatedly knocked material back, often for reasons she couldn't explain, and yet expected him to keep on having another go, rarely offering additional monies for his trouble, reflected how unaware she was that this was a professionals' game and made her look more and more like some office manager pretending to be a movie producer.

He shut these dispiriting thoughts from his mind and trudged on.

They went upstairs to the bedrooms, which they'd all now investigated for themselves and settled in. These were exclusively comfortable, well-furnished and with large double-sized beds; each one even had its own colour scheme. Thankfully, Turner didn't detect any evil presence here. Surprisingly though, it was the same story on the next floor up – in the attic/observatory; a strange octagonal chamber that had been used in *Daemonia* for one of its infamous Black Mass sequences. This room, which still retained its domed glass ceiling and gazed up at a glacial winter sky, had also been adapted into a bedroom, though in this case the bed was a four-poster. The floor, once painted white with cavorting black devil-figures inscribed on it, was now carpeted and the walls were tastefully papered and hung with pictures. Rick found its atmosphere eerie, but that was undoubtedly because of the associations the place held for him. In the film, the walls had been jet-black, while some chemical had been used in the large stone hearth so that when logs were stacked there and set alight, they burned with a searing crimson flame.

"Nothing up here?" Wilkes wondered.

Turner shook his head. "No more than anywhere else. I've a feeling that whatever lurks in this house, lurks in the very fabric of it. Whatever was summoned here, soaked itself into the soul of the building … like a stain, an indelible stain."

Rick made a mental note to remember this as a possible title for the film – *The Stain*.

"You actually believe something was summoned then?" Tanya asked.

"It's just a turn of phrase, Mrs Wilkes."

"Fielding, please."

"Sorry, Mrs Fielding. Whatever it is, though, it isn't native to this site."

"And it's not specific to this room?" Roni felt it necessary to ask again, presumably because she couldn't think of a more original question.

The medium shook his head. "No. But I think bad things have happened in here." He glanced at Wilkes. "Am I correct?"

"Simulated bad things, yes."

As Rick recollected, for a movie that had had the swinging '60s written all over it, the Black Mass scene filmed in this room had been quite shocking. Among other things it had featured a sacrificial victim who was slowly mutilated to death, but only after a vile and highly sacrilegious mockery of the Holy Eucharist. A demonic being had then appeared, a hulking, misshapen brute – a patchwork thing, rather like a crude combination of Leatherface from *The Texas Chainsaw Massacre* and Jason from *Friday 13th* – which had proceeded to rape its way through the gathered acolytes. The censors had taken particular offence at close-ups of men and women's faces written with joyous rapture as they were viciously and repeatedly violated. With all this in mind, Rick wondered if there might, after all, be something in what Tanya had said earlier on; about wicked acts – even simulated acts – that were so aberrant, so defiant of God's law that something truly horrible might emerge from them. For the first time that weekend he began to think that they might get a decent script out of this after all.

*

"You've not had much to say for yourself," Rick commented, finding Gail alone in the kitchen. It was now after ten o'clock, and the rest of the team were gathered in the lounge, where Turner was holding a thus far uneventful séance.

The secretary smiled and continued with the washing-up. They'd had sandwiches that evening rather than a slap-up meal, but there'd still been one or two dishes to clean, and when Gail had volunteered to go and do it – as she no doubt did with the office tea-things every day back at Pinewood – no-one had objected.

"Don't enjoy communing with the dead?" he wondered.

"No. Just a bit out of my depth," she replied.

"How do you mean?"

"Intellectually."

"What, among this lot? I hope you're joking."

"Listen," Gail said loftily, "Stafford Wilkes is a great man. Or so Roni keeps informing me."

Rick sniggered. "And I bet she tells you this in a disappointed tone, as though she's desperately trying to widen your education but not having much success, yeah?"

"You got it."

Rick leaned on the cabinets beside her. "The irony is, of course, that you probably know more about this place than the rest of us put together."

Gail looked surprised. "Me?"

"You come from the South Coast, don't you?"

"Yeah, Southampton. But that's twenty miles away."

"You must have heard of Godley Grange before?"

"Not really."

"Well … you must have heard of the New Forest?"

She gave him a look. "I have, as it happens, heard of the New Forest."

"Devil worshippers' playground, isn't it? Least, that's what I'm told."

She shrugged and began to insert dishes into the drying rack. "There are stories, but there are stories everywhere. You're from East Anglia, aren't you?"

"Me? London … Edgware."

"I mean before that."

He nodded and grinned. "Yeah. Moved to the smoke in '94. My accent's still that strong, huh?"

"Guttural. Almost unintelligible."

"Cheers."

"East Anglia's witch country too, isn't it?" she said. "Matthew Hopkins, *Witchfinder General* and all that."

Rick pondered. "Suppose so. But that was a long time ago. *Daemonia*'s less than forty years old."

"*Daemonia*." Gail shook her head, as if it was all so much nonsense. "Don't know what my old dad would say if he knew I was involved in something like this."

Rick remembered being told that Gail's deceased father had once been an active member of the National Viewers' and Listeners' Association, which was indeed ironic considering the nature of *this* project.

"Bloody awful film anyway," she added. "We watched it the other night. Didn't scare me at all."

Rick sighed. "That's the challenge facing us, to be honest. Don't think anyone scares easily these days."

At which point, entirely of its own volition, the door to the cellar swung open.

They regarded it in silence.

Then walked over to it together and peeked down the dank, stone stairwell. The lights were on at the bottom. Rick wanted to laugh, but suddenly there was a creep at the back of his neck. Gail, practical as ever, tested the door, swinging it back and forth on its hinges. It was actually quite stiff; when it moved, it made an arthritic creak.

"Strange," she said.

"Suppose we should go down and take a look," Rick replied.

She glanced at him in a humouring sort of way. "You absolutely sure about that?"

"It's what we're here for, isn't it? Tanya wants us to experience weird phenomena and draw inspiration from it."

Gail's noncommittal grunt spoke volumes about what she thought of Tanya.

They went down the stair side-by-side. Because it was below the damp-course, it was colder down there than in the rest of the house, but now, oddly, they found it considerably colder than it had been earlier. Rick was surprised to see their breath pluming out in translucent clouds.

They moved warily from one area to the next. The hard electric light left no corner hidden. In fact, at times it showed them more than they wanted to see: mouse droppings along the skirting boards, a rolled-up carpet that was green and slimy with mould, an overhead web in which there hung a spider the size of a human glove. When they reached the central room – the one where the famous beating-to-death sequence had been filmed – they paused again and listened.

"Must have been a draft of wind," Gail finally said.

"There's no wind down here," Rick replied.

"Well, that door was quite stiff. It didn't open on its own."

"Let's not get carried away. This is an old building. Old buildings are full of strange things."

"Doors that open on their own?"

"It's freezing outside," Rick offered. "Metal and wood both warp when it freezes."

"Yeah, but it's been freezing for two weeks. They should already have warped."

Rick had to chuckle at the irrefutable logic of such an observation. It broke the ice a little. Perhaps it was time to get a grip: all that had really happened was that a door had swung open.

And now another one did.

At the far end of the chamber, about seven yards ahead of them, located behind several propped-up planks, a door they hadn't previously noticed clicked off its catch and squeaked backward a couple of inches.

There was no light on the other side of this one, only blackness.

At first Rick and Gail said nothing; merely stared at it, expecting someone to come out. Whereas the previous incident might conceivably have been caused by a blast of wind, there was something deliberate and mechanical about the way *this* door had been opened: the manner in which it had unlatched itself; the way it had only swung back several inches and then stopped as though someone on the other side wanted to peer out.

Unconsciously, Gail was now gripping Rick's wrist. "Do we really need to go and check this one?" she said.

"We should do."

"How about if I stay here?"

"Not a bad idea. Be like *The House on Haunted Hill*."

"What do you mean?"

"The old version. You know … the Vincent Price one. When the guy and the girl get separated in the cellar. He goes knocking on walls in another room. She waits there on her own, and this hideous hag comes out of the darkness, claws outstretched."

"In that case I'll come with you."

"And there we were, saying it wasn't easy to get scared these days."

"Your words, not mine."

They ventured forward. The darkness beyond this second open door was as impenetrable as any darkness they'd ever seen. Despite the numbing cold, there was a strong, rather unpleasant scent – rot, decay? Wordlessly, they moved the obstructing planks, and pushed the door open properly. The recess behind it was clearly a room of some sort – it was too large to be a closet – but still nothing was visible inside. Again, Rick had the hair-raising notion that they were being watched from in there.

"Can't see a bloody thing," he mumbled.

"Here." Gail pushed something into his hand. "Try this."

He glanced down and saw a cigarette lighter. "Didn't know you smoked?"

"I don't. But we brought candles and stuff in case there was a power cut, this being an old house and all."

"Very efficient."

"That's me."

He struck the lighter and held it up.

In the wavering luminescence, they saw a bare brick chamber about the size of a lavatory cubicle, though there was no lavatory inside it. A pair of rusted pipes crossed the ceiling, both encased in wads of dust-thick cobweb. There was nothing else in there except green stains down the walls, and, directly facing them, a lengthy piece of odiously stained sacking, which hung from a single nail.

"How disappointing," Gail said, sounding relieved.

Rick found himself staring at the length of sacking. "Who were you expecting, *Dracula: Prince of Darkness*?"

"I don't know. Let's just get away from here, eh?"

She moved her hand from his wrist to his elbow, forcibly turned him round and steered him back across the main cellar room. They left it without a backward glance, walking increasingly quickly down the adjoining corridor. But they were halfway up the stair, when Rick suddenly stopped and said that he had to go back.

She looked at him askance. "What?"

"There's something I have to check on."

"Back down there?"

"I'm afraid so."

"Would you be offended if I said that this time you were on your own?"

"Not at all." And he shook his head stiffly.

She continued up. "I'll put the kettle on, so you've got something to look forward to."

He nodded a wry 'thank-you', turned and descended again. Moving back along the cellar passage, he tried not to look at the packing cases and jumbled furniture lying to left and right. When he re-entered the main chamber, he did his best not to glance down at the floor to see if traces of the old pentangle were still visible under the rags and rubbish. Instead, he focussed on the open doorway to that tiny, bare room. Though, of course, it hadn't *really* been bare, had it? That thing hanging in there – he couldn't be sure, but had it actually been a bag made of sacking? A bag of burlap sacking possibly? Could it be the very same burlap sack the murder victim had been tied up in all those years ago when beaten with clubs in that terrifyingly violent scene? Those brackish stains that covered it – could they be blood, or whatever the effects people had used for blood back in 1969?

It shouldn't be here. Not after all this time. If it was, it was a truly remarkable find, and they simply had to use it in the new movie. But in all honesty, it shouldn't be here. And now he was inexplicably frightened that, when he looked again, it *wouldn't* be.

He approached the black doorway, which still stood open as though waiting for him. And then realised that he'd given the lighter back to Gail. Which meant he'd have to go bodily into that cubicle – that dark cubicle with its foul stench – and take the thing down with his bare hands. And he wasn't at all sure he could do that.

And then – *CRASH!* – the door slammed closed.

Right in his face.

Just before he reached it.

Without hesitation, without a second thought, Rick whirled around and ran back across the room, swerving out into the corridor. Behind him, there was another explosion of sound, as though some great heap of junk had been thrown over. Then there were two *thuds* – he imagined feet alighting on the floor. A scuffling followed, as though those feet were racing after him.

With barely suppressed shouts, Rick threw himself up the stair, taking three treads at a time. He half expected the door at the top also to bang closed in his face. But it didn't.

Mercifully, it didn't.

*

Rick didn't say anything about what had happened down in the cellar.

Firstly, he wasn't sure he actually believed it. And secondly, he regarded himself as the most rational person in the building, and it simply wouldn't do if *he* was the first one to start panicking. Of course, it wasn't easy keeping quiet like this, especially in front of Gail, who'd noticed immediately on his re-appearance from below that something was wrong. She'd pointed out that he looked flustered, that his hands were shaking. He'd replied that it was nothing: he'd slipped on the stair and given his back a twinge.

To worsen things, Tanya managed to make him feel guilty. Her fireside séance had been an abject failure. Even with Wallace Turner present, they hadn't gained any response from the spirit world, much to their hostess's disappointment. She was now handing out notebooks and pens to everyone, advising they keep them on their bedside tables so they could write down anything suspicious that happened during the hours of darkness. It all seemed very amateurish by normal ghost hunting standards. Where were the heat-seeking cameras, the EMF meters, the thermometers and infrared motion-detectors? It made Rick realise how much of a shot in the dark this weekend actually was. But he still didn't say anything.

As they ascended to the bedrooms, he felt weary and confused. It had been a long day and sleep was already nagging at him, but he suspected it wouldn't come easily. With most of the lights off, the gaunt emptiness of the sprawling manor house, especially its downstairs, now seemed far more oppressive than it had before.

"We all know which rooms we're in," Tanya said, turning on the landing to face them.

There were grunts in the affirmative. They'd all been allocated accommodation along the same central passage, and each had found his or her room satisfactory when stowing their baggage earlier.

"I'm in the green room," Roni confirmed.

"I'm in the gold," Gail said.

Tanya nodded. "If anyone needs us, Stafford and I are in the blue."

"Red," Turner added.

"Purple for me," Graham said. "It's a bit like a funeral parlour, but what the hell."

That only left Rick. "Oh … beige, I suppose."

Tanya glanced at Turner. "Anything new yet?"

He'd been around the house one last time, on his own, before they'd all come upstairs. He'd even popped down to the cellar but hadn't reported anything strange or out of place. He again shook his head, seemingly puzzled. "This atmosphere is quiet at the moment. But I'd be very surprised if there wasn't some activity later in the night."

The tone of his voice was low and rather uneasy, which, after the business below, Rick now found ominous rather than comical. Once again, he thought of the empty rooms downstairs, all lying in obsidian blackness. A second passed as the rest of them contemplated this. Then, one by one, they said their goodnights. Rick was surprised to see Tanya come straight over to him.

"And how are *you* doing?" she asked.

"I'm sorry?"

"Any thrilling thoughts yet that we can translate into a superb script?"

"Well … one or two scenarios have suggested themselves."

She seemed pleased with that. "Tomorrow afternoon, me, you and Stafford will get our heads together and thrash out a cracking synopsis. It'll be the best we've ever done."

It'll be the *first* you've ever done, he thought to himself, but he didn't say it.

Rick's bedroom door was located between Graham and Gail's. Gail was standing alongside hers as he made to go in.

"Glad I've got you for a neighbour," she said. For the first time, the level-headed secretary seemed a little anxious. Her body language was tense, her smile forced.

Rick understood why. He peered up and down the landing passage. It was done exclusively in dark mahogany panels. Even the carpet was a deep brown. The little light, provided by shaded bulbs interspersed between gaps of thirty metres or more, was largely absorbed by this sombre décor. He glanced back at the girl and decided not to tell her that he too was on-edge. Instead, he affected a cheeky grin. "Anything you need, just knock on my wall."

"I'm not sure that'd do any good," she replied. "This place is solid stone."

"Find the secret doorway then. Come in to see me that way."

"Oh yeah!" she retorted. "Like in *The Cat and the Canary*? Now that one really did scare me, even though it had Bob Hope in it. Bodies in wardrobes, maniacs wandering around in face-paint and bloodstained shrouds."

"Hmmm," Rick agreed. "Better forget the secret door."

"If I need you, don't worry … you'll hear me," she said.

He nodded and smiled again. "I'll keep an ear open."

They went into their separate rooms, the doors clicking closed behind them. Gail was such a pleasant person beneath that prim exterior that Rick would very much have liked her to come in and see him. Not for sexual reasons – he loved Shirley dearly – but because she was fun to be with and would provide reassuring company on what was likely to be a long, desolate night. He surveyed his bedroom before stripping down to his boxer shorts. In the low lamplight, it looked even more sumptuous, more opulent than it had during the day. The big bed would undoubtedly be comfortable and warm. However, the huge hearth facing it was bare: just an arch of sooty brick. It was probably never used now that there was central heating in the building. It would be nice though, he thought as he climbed into bed, to see a roaring fire there. He imagined the orange reflections on the walls and tapestries.

And indeed, as Rick slipped surprisingly quickly into sleep, that was what he dreamed about: *dancing, glowing shapes; cavorting red phantoms on all sides of him.*

He woke abruptly and sat up. His body was slick with sweat and now chilled in the ice-cold darkness. The heating had likely gone off. Doubtless it would only come back on around five or six in the morning. But what had woken him? What had he just heard?

He heard it again.

Muffled movements far below.

In the cellar perhaps?

A loud but distant *thud*, as of furniture being flung over. And then feet. Heavy, booted feet. Thumping angrily up the cellar stair.

At first the footfalls were down in the subterranean depths of the house, but now they were rapidly ascending.

Rick felt his flesh goose-pimple.

With a horrendous *CRASH*, the pounding feet burst from the cellar door and into the kitchen. There was a split-second of silence, then a renewed banging and thumping as they started to rove at speed around the downstairs, seemingly running from one room to the next. At last, inevitably, they came to the main stairway in the hall, and charged up it. *Dum DUM dum DUM dum DUM* ... their volume was thunderous, the impacts reverberating through the building. Whoever the perpetrator was, he was of enormous stature and hugely powerful.

Rick leaped from the bed. His hand reached out for the lampstand, which, not surprisingly, he couldn't find in the blackness. He heard the feet reach the top of the stair and turn unhesitatingly into this passage, which they now began to run down, heading straight – and somehow, he knew this automatically – towards *his* door.

Unable to find the light, he scrabbled down beside the bed where he'd dumped his holdall. He rummaged around inside it, discarding clothes and loose toiletries.

The feet were maybe twenty yards away. They sounded larger than ever. Now they were fifteen yards. Now ten.

Rick dug frantically in the bag, not even sure what he was looking for. But then his hand located something: a cylinder of smooth metal. He realised it was an aerosol; his aftershave. Not appreciating at the time how absurdly useless a piece of weaponry this might be, he snatched it up and advanced with it until he was three yards from the door. The feet had arrived on the other side of it.

And had immediately halted.

There was an ear-deadening silence. But it would only last a second or so. Any moment now, Rick expected an astonishing blow to fall on the door itself. The entire thing would be kicked through with smashing force.

But there was nothing. And the seconds ticked past.

Rick grew colder and stiffer in the darkness. Until at last, when he couldn't stand it anymore, he moved forward, holding the aerosol directly in front of him, fully intending to eject its spray into the eyes of whoever the intruder might be. Slowly but determinedly, he reached for the door-handle, turned it … and yanked the door open.

And somebody *was* on the other side.

It was Graham, in a t-shirt and tracksuit pants. He was sallow-faced and bog-eyed, as though he'd just been sleeping, and he jumped with fright to have the door opened right in front of him. By the looks of it, he'd been about to knock.

"What the hell are you doing here?" Rick demanded, not lowering the can.

Graham shook his head dully. "Sorry … I wondered if you'd just heard something?"

"Have you been downstairs?"

"Eh? No, course not. I wondered if …"

"I heard you the first time." Rick was still suspicious but dropped the aerosol to his side. "What time is it?"

"Er … two-fifteen."

"Two-fifteen." Rick considered. He'd been asleep for little more than an hour. "I did hear something, yeah."

"Like whispering voices?"

Rick stared at him. "What do you mean 'voices'?"

"Like two people walking along this passage, whispering?"

Rick stared at him all the harder. If Tanya's gofer was lying, he was doing a good job of concealing it. "No, that's not what I heard," Rick finally answered. And he described the pounding footfalls, only for Graham to shake his head blankly.

"I didn't hear anything like that. Surely, I *would* have done. I'm only next door?"

"Tell me about these 'whispering voices'."

"It was like a … well, a furtive conversation."

"Could it have been two of the others, going to the bathroom maybe?"

Graham shook his head. "I didn't recognise them, if it was. They were sniggering, having a joke. It was a bit unpleasant, to be honest."

Rick pondered. "Okay. Let me get some clothes on, and we'll look around."

A minute later they were back in the passage, fully dressed. There was silence from the other bedrooms.

"So, what do you think, do we wake people up?" Graham wondered.

Rick didn't reply. He'd just spotted something. He nodded and pointed. Graham turned, and he saw it too. At the extreme end of the corridor there was an alcove covered by a maroon curtain. Even as they zeroed in on it, that curtain moved. Only slightly; it didn't ripple or billow the way it might in a draft. It twitched, as though someone had nudged it from the other side.

Rick mouthed an instruction, and Graham nodded. They moved down the passage as stealthily as they could. At the curtain they paused, listening intently. There was no sound. Then they lunged forward, ripping the material aside – and were astounded by the sight of Wallace Turner, the eyes bulging in his grizzled face, his hair a frenzied mop.

With a wild shriek, he flung himself at them. "We've got to get out of here! We've all got to get out!"

Instinctively, they caught hold of him, trying to wrestle him to a standstill. But he was so panic-stricken that, wiry as he was, he brought all three of them to the floor. By this time other doors in the passage were opening. One by one, the rest of the team poked their heads out, some still fuddled with sleep.

"You don't understand," Turner jabbered. "It's stirring, it's waking up. And you can't even comprehend it …"

He'd clambered back to his feet, but not before Rick had noticed that his breath was foetid with alcohol and that he was wearing the same shabby clothes as earlier, which suggested that he hadn't yet been to bed. Turner stumbled away from them but caromed backward from a wall; what looked like a hipflask fell from his pocket.

Tanya had emerged onto the landing, clad in a diaphanous nightgown that trailed behind her almost regally. "What the hell is going on?" she demanded. "Mr Turner?"

"We've got to leave!" he told her. "We have to! I've seen it. I only caught a glimpse, but it's here … it's all over this atmosphere, and it's utterly foul!"

The entire group had now gathered, but before anyone else could speak there was a sound from overhead. They glanced up at the ceiling. It was a dragging sound, like something extraordinarily heavy being moved across wood. A cacophonous *BANG* followed it, and then an explosion of breaking glass.

"What the devil is going on here?" Tanya breathed. She'd blanched a little, as had several of the others. At last, they too were being exposed to the mysteries of Godley Grange, and all of a sudden it didn't seem quite so exciting.

"It's the observatory," Wilkes replied. He glanced around at them. "Isn't it? That's the only room above us."

"Correct," Rick said, a chill down his spine. "Someone's in the observatory."

"Under no circumstances go up there," Turner moaned. He was leaning against a wall, and now dropped his head into his brown, spider-like hands. "Don't … don't do it!"

There was another shocking impact overhead.

"We've got to check it," Rick said.

"No!" Turner threw himself forward. His odd yellow eyes were bloodshot; whether or not that was through drinking was unclear, but it was a disturbing sight. He

grabbed Rick by the collar and thrust him back. Then he turned and did the same with Tanya. "It wants us to stay, but we mustn't. It's setting traps for us."

And then, in the space of a second, Turner wilted.

It was like watching a flower on speeded-up film. Without another word, he seemed to fold on himself, drop to his knees and sag sideways. He fell heavily and lifelessly to the carpet. Gail, who was still in her pyjamas, knelt quickly beside him. As a permanent carer for her mother before the ailing lady had been put into a hospice, she'd picked up numerous nursing techniques, and was now Lionheart Productions' official first aider. She hurriedly checked Turner's vital signs: his pulse – not just in his wrist, but in his neck – then his breathing. She felt around the base of his skull, and down his spine.

"I think he's fainted," she said. "But for all I know he could just be drunk."

"Well that was money well spent," Wilkes observed.

"What do we do?" Roni asked.

She'd come out from her room in a knee-length t-shirt, and of course hadn't had time to put her slap on. Her normally coiffed hair was in total disarray. As such, she looked markedly less glamorous than usual. She also looked frightened, much more so than the others; she was white-faced with it.

"What do we do?" she asked again, producing a cigarette from somewhere and nervously lighting it.

"We'd better get him onto his bed," Gail said. "It looks safe to move him."

The men picked Turner up – he wasn't especially heavy anyway – and carted him into his room. As Rick had suspected, the bed in there was unruffled, the coverlet still in place. They dumped him down on it and stood back.

Gail came in after them. “The only thing is,” she said, “do we call an ambulance? I mean I’m not an expert, and the guy’s unconscious. What do you all think?”

Wilkes, impressive in a quilted silk dressing-gown, bent over and examined Turner closely. When he finally straightened up again, he was frowning. “He’s not unconscious, Gail, darling. He’s asleep. You were right before – he’s a wretched drunk. And a fraud, no doubt.”

“I’m not sure about that,” Tanya said. “What about upstairs?”

They exchanged tense glances. There was no noise overhead now, but the sounds they’d heard previously had been like bombs going off.

“He …” Roni finally said, her voice quavering. “Mr Turner said there was something foul up there.” She took another drag on her cigarette. Her hand was shaking like a leaf. Graham touched her shoulder to try and console her, but she flinched away from him.

“Before we even contemplate the possibility that Mr Turner was telling the truth,” Rick advised, “let’s consider the more likely alternatives.”

“Like what?” Tanya asked.

“Like burglars,” he replied. “We’ve been hearing unexplained noises for the past few minutes now. Anywhere else, we’d assume this meant that someone had broken in.”

“He’s right,” Wilkes said, tightening the knot on the cord of his gown. “I vote we look around, and our first port of call must undoubtedly be the observatory.”

There was yet another silence. No-one was in a rush to volunteer, but they all understood that it needed to be done. They chose weapons: Wilkes took a poker from the fireplace in his bedroom; Graham pulled down the curtain over the alcove and extricated its brass rail; Rick, finally realising how nonsensical it'd been to opt for an aerosol spray, took a sock and filled it with loose change until it was as heavy as a gangland cosh. Then the three men went upstairs. The women, who though they all regarded themselves as members of London's intellectual elite, were on this occasion happy to let chauvinism take its course and brought up the rear.

The observatory was accessible by a narrow, winding stairway, which during daytime would be bathed in sunshine from an overhead skylight, but at night was a black spiral. Nevertheless, they proceeded up it, silent and bunched together. At the top, the doorway to the observatory stood wide open. Frosted moonlight filled the spacious room beyond it from the overhead dome. At this ungodly hour it didn't reveal a great deal, though *one* thing was quite clear: the observatory had been trashed.

Broken ornaments lay scattered on the carpet. Every item of furniture, even the heavy four-posted bed, had been overturned.

At last, Wilkes found the light switch and turned it on, which brought additional macabre detail to their attention. Previously plump upholstery had been slashed and gutted. There were daubings on the walls in some vile black substance: to Rick they resembled the runic symbols from *Night Of The Demon*, though they were so crude and unclear they could also have been attempted recreations of the devil-figures painted on the floor for Wilkes' original Black Mass scene. More worrying than any of this, though, were the shapes laid out in the centre of the room. These had been formed from folded bedsheets. The sheets themselves were pristine, not damaged in any way. But it was the shapes they made that were so significant.

They were human coffins.

And there were seven of them: one for each person present.

*

"It seems a bit cowardly," Graham said, "all of us spending the night together in the same room, with the lights on."

He, Rick and Wilkes were now back in the lounge, where a great pile of bedding, including pillows and quilts, had been heaped on one of the sofas. They were all three of them dressed again. Wilkes had even re-donned his immaculate three-piece suit.

"It's not what they normally do in horror movies," the big man acknowledged, warming his back on the fire, a fresh cigar in his hand.

At which point the three women came in, also dressed. "Turner's out for the count," Tanya said irritably. "Can't wake him for love nor money, the drunken sot. Might as well leave him up there …" Her words tailed off as she stared across the room towards the fire. Then she exploded: *"What the buggering hell's going on!"*

Startled, the three men stepped aside as she scuttled her way through them.

"This is all the paperwork we needed for this weekend!" she shouted, dropping to her knees in front of the flames. "There are copies of the original *Daemonia* script in there!"

For the first time the men noticed that, as well as logs, the fire was feeding on a wad of documents. Roni dashed out through the hall to the dining room, to check, but she was back shortly afterwards to solemnly confirm that the papers on the fire were indeed those that Tanya had brought in her briefcase.

"Who's the God-damned genius responsible for this?" Tanya demanded, only managing to scrape out a few blackened fragments.

Rick and Wilkes turned to Graham, who had been the first one to come back downstairs after they'd decided to spend the remainder of the night in the lounge. His response was immediate and defensive: "Don't look at me. The fire was already going when I got here. I assumed one of you lot had come down before me and lit it."

No-one replied. Now that they considered it, Graham had only been a minute ahead of the rest. As the fire had been extinguished when they'd first gone up to bed, he couldn't possibly have had time to make up a new one and bring it to this kind of blaze.

Tanya kneeled back and shook her head. "Stafford, we're going to have to go back to Pinewood. We can't carry on here without …"

And once again her words tailed off. She was peering through the flames to something on the other side. A second passed, then she leaned forward until her face was almost in the fire. When she finally turned and stood up, her cheeks and forehead had visibly reddened. "Which of you is responsible for this?" she said in a hoarse whisper.

Wilkes took his cigar out. "What's the matter?"

"Stafford, if this is your idea of a joke …"

Roni approached her. "Tanya?"

Tanya jerked away. “Get back from me, you bitch! Did *you* do this?”

Roni looked stunned. “I don’t know what you mean.”

And then, abruptly, Tanya’s façade of cold outrage seemed to break, and horror and grief came flooding through. She clasped a hand to her brow and her shoulders heaved as she started to sob. “It’s not …” she stammered, “… no-one else could know … I don’t see how …” She looked up again. Tears stained her cheeks, but she was now wild-eyed.

“Tanya, what’s happened?” Roni asked.

“Get back!” Tanya snapped. “I’m not staying here a moment longer. This place is evil, do you hear me! *Evil!*”

And she fled, crashing out from the lounge, and, by the sounds of it, running across the hall into the dining room, the door of which she slammed closed behind her. A second later she began to sob again, loud enough for them all to hear her.

They gazed at each other, dumbstruck. Roni and Gail finally went stumbling from the room in pursuit of her. Wilkes seemed as puzzled as anyone; his cigar hung limply between two fingers. Rick turned to the fire. He crouched and looked into it, and immediately spotted something strange. At the back of the hearth, written with a fingertip in the thick soot that had crusted there, was a single sentence. It read:

Jeanette says ‘Hi’

He told the others. Graham came over and checked for himself. Wilkes stood stock-still, though the information affected him. He noticeably paled. With slow, mechanical movements, he began to puff on his cigar again.

"What does it mean?" Graham asked. "Stafford?"

Wilkes cleared his throat awkwardly. "What it means is, er … er, is that this building is genuinely haunted."

The younger men glanced at each other, perplexed.

"Perhaps I should explain," Wilkes said. "I can't be sure of course, but 'Jeanette' is almost certainly a reference to Jeanette Sandyford. She was a young woman whom Tanya used to work with in her former occupation."

"At Shadwell & Bakerville?" Graham said.

Wilkes nodded. "Tanya held a middle management post at Shadwell & Bakerville. That was an accountancy firm in the City. One of her underlings was a rather difficult girl called Jeanette Sandyford. She wasn't really able to do her job and she caused a number of problems."

Rick already had a sneaking feeling that this was only going to be *one* side of the story.

"Tanya did her best for the girl," Wilkes added.

I'll bet she did, Rick thought.

"But it was a lost cause." Wilkes paused to try and remember. "As I understand it, other things were going wrong in this Jeanette Sandyford's life. She had a miscarriage, and her husband left her as a result. Shortly after this, her mother died. At length, she took to drink. Quite heavily. She was sent home from the office a couple of times under the influence. Eventually, Tanya had no option but to suspend her from work, and the following weekend … well, the girl died. She wrecked her car somewhere between London and Brighton. She was well over the limit at the time, but there was a suggestion it might have been suicide. Ridiculous though it is, Tanya's felt guilty ever since. It's the main reason she decided to leave Shadwell & Bakerville."

Rick wondered if the truth was more a case of *someone else* deciding that Tanya ought to leave. Perhaps because she'd been more complicit in this poor girl's demise than Wilkes was admitting to? Office bullies came in all shapes and forms, and Rick could easily envisage a pretty sylphlike one.

"Anyway," Wilkes said grimly, "the point is that no-one else knows that story. At least, no one here … apart from Tanya and me. Which rather suggests that whoever wrote that message is party to extremely personal information." He glanced at Rick with an odd half-grin. "It's rather like the little girl in *The Exorcist* telling the priest private things about his mother, wouldn't you say?"

For the moment, Rick was unconcerned with cinematic references. "I don't suppose anyone else knew we were coming here? I mean anyone from Tanya's former life?"

Wilkes shook his head. "We've kept the whole thing under wraps, as you know."

And that was true. They'd all been sworn to secrecy about this weekend, because Wilkes only wanted to launch his publicity machine when the movie was in the bag. Of course, just because he wanted it that way didn't mean that everyone was playing ball.

Rick crouched again and stared at the sooty scrawl. Whoever had done this certainly knew about Tanya's past, and they'd put her personal paperwork on the fire to ensure that she was the first person who'd spot it. It was undoubtedly a nasty trick, and the work of a clever, calculating mind.

Roni re-entered. They could still hear Tanya crying in the dining room, and Gail trying to console her. However, Roni was more her old self. Spying an opportunity to get even further into Tanya's good books, she'd determinedly pulled herself together. "Stafford," she said in a clipped tone, "Tanya wants to leave. She's frightened and upset, and she wants to leave."

Wilkes contemplated this. "Understandable, I suppose."

"I've volunteered to drive her into Brockenhurst," Roni added. "It's the nearest town and we should be able to find a hotel there, or a pub where we can get a room."

The movie maker nodded gravely.

"I'll go too," Graham said, reaching for his jacket.

"Oh no … no I'm sorry, Graham," Wilkes said quite firmly. "I need you here."

"You need *me*?" Graham looked nonplussed.

Wilkes nodded, but offered no explanation.

Rick felt he understood why. Graham's curious relationship with Tanya had not escaped her husband's notice after all.

"So, is it all right?" Roni asked. "I mean, if I take Tanya? You'll still have a vehicle here should you guys need to make a sharp exit."

That was correct – there were two cars here at present, Rick's Allegro and Roni's Datsun – but Wilkes seemed amused by the very notion that they too might need to escape from Godley Grange. "Don't worry, we won't be going anywhere," he said, "we have a movie to write."

Now Gail appeared in the doorway. "Tanya's ready to go," she said awkwardly. "She won't stay here a minute longer."

"Do you intend to leave us too, my dear?" Wilkes asked her. "You can if you wish."

Gail looked from one to the other. "It's okay … I'll stay."

"I'm most grateful."

They moved out into the hall, where Tanya stood in something like a daze. She was white-faced and red-eyed, a shocked shadow of the bustling, efficient woman she normally was. As Roni helped her on with her waxed coat, she barely spoke.

Wilkes unlocked the heavy front door.

On the way out, Tanya stopped. She spoke briefly and quietly with her husband, then shook her head, perhaps resisting a last-ditch attempt to get her to stay. A minute later, they were all out on the steps. The night was bone-numbingly cold. A thick blanket of mist had come down and lay over the carpet of snow; in the glare of the Datsun's headlights, it rolled and twisted in fantastical shapes.

Rick whispered quietly to Gail: "Brave of you. This is a scary development."

She pursed her lips. "If you want the truth, I'm not sure they'll find any lodgings at this hour. Brockenhurst is smaller in real life than it looks on a map."

The Datsun pulled away, its tyres crunching on the frosted gravel. Roni and Tanya were little more than huddled shapes inside it.

As Wilkes watched it draw off along the drive, he chugged on his cigar again. The departure of his wife didn't seem to have especially lowered his spirits. "Gail, dear," he rumbled. "Any chance of coffee? Should give us the energy boost we need."

She looked surprised. "You want an energy boost at three in the morning?"

"Absolutely." He grinned through wreathes of cigar smoke. "As I say, we have a movie to write." And he went back indoors.

Gail glanced at Rick, shrugged and followed her boss.

Graham stayed where he was, scowling. "I think this is getting a bit beyond a joke, working us at this hour."

Rick was indifferent. "We're all awake. Why delay?"

Graham, whose real irritation possibly stemmed from his not being allowed to accompany Tanya, shook his head bitterly. "I've never known Stafford do anything like this before. He's turned into a bloody slave-driver."

"Maybe something's pissed him off."

"What do you mean?"

Rick stared at him. "What do you think I mean?"

Suddenly Graham looked frightened. "You don't think he suspects there's something going on between me and Tanya? Because there's not."

"Whatever."

"No, there really isn't." Graham had become quite animated. "She's a good-looking woman, but she's way too old for me."

"So, what exactly are you doing with her?"

"I work for her."

"What, as a professional office boy?"

"Yeah."

"On a micro-salary, no doubt?"

"Yeah. So?"

"And you're happy with that?" Rick had trouble keeping the scorn out of his voice. "I mean, I'm sorry

Graham, but I'm not buying it. You've got 'fortune hunter' written all over you."

Graham stiffened. At first, he said nothing, but then he admitted: "Okay, I want to be in films. Is that such a crime?"

"And you think she's going to make you a star?"

"She said she would."

"And you still insist there's nothing going on between you?"

"Nothing. On my mother's grave."

Ironically, Rick was now starting to believe it, because suddenly he could see a bigger picture. Tanya was evidently the driving force in this relationship. She found Graham attractive, handsome, rugged. In short, she fancied him rotten, and thought that, as well as making an opening for him in the film business, she could probably make an opening for him in her personal life – but only when she was sufficiently secure in her new role as movie mogul for Stafford to be dispensed with. Until then she was keeping him on ice. Not that life was ever that simple, of course, as a procession of ambitious amateurs had discovered over the years.

"Sorry to spoil your illusions, pal," Rick said, "but you're dreaming. First of all, I very much doubt these people will even get a movie onto the studio floor, let alone into the cinemas. Stafford's finished, and Tanya doesn't have a clue what she's doing. Secondly, even if they *do* manage it, Stafford's got you marked as someone who's been banging, or at least trying to bang, his wife. You really think he's going to help you carve out a career path to Hollywood?"

"So, why's he keeping me around?"

"It's a puzzle, I admit. But then everything about tonight is a puzzle."

Before they could speak further, a resounding *thump* – like a heavy impact on metal – filled the frozen night. The two men glanced uncertainly around, finally focussing on a dull, yellow glow perhaps two hundred yards into the gloom-filled forest.

"What's that?" Graham wondered. "Fire?"

"I'll tell you what that is," Rick said slowly. "It's the car. Jesus Christ, I think they've just crashed."

*

The car wasn't actually burning, as they'd first feared.

The dull glow they'd seen was the glow of its reversing lights filtered through layers of icy mist. The vehicle had not collided with any unyielding object but seemed to have run into a snowdrift on the left-hand side of the drive, where its front wheels had buried themselves to the arches. It was angled diagonally across the narrow roadway, completely blocking it and could not, apparently, be moved. Roni was pointlessly revving the thing when the others arrived. When they knocked on the driver's window, she screamed and tried to grab hold of Tanya, who was cowering in the front passenger seat. But then she recognised them, and, sobbing with relief, clambered frantically into their arms.

Tanya was in no less a distraught state. When they helped her out, she was crying fresh tears and moaning repeatedly: "Never going to let us leave, never going to let us leave …"

Wilkes and Gail put an extra coat around her and helped her back towards the house.

"What the hell happened?" Graham asked Roni. He was a sturdy lad, but the girl clung to him with both hands around his neck, making it doubly difficult for him to steer her back in the right direction.

"Something … something was in the road," she stuttered. "It was like a snowman, only the most evil fucking snowman I've ever seen."

"Come on, Roni," Graham said, "how can a snowman be evil?"

"It was grinning. Horribly. It had icicles for teeth, and its eyes were like human eyes – all crossed and bloody, like they'd been gouged out of someone's head."

Rick and Graham listened to her, astonished, but by her flowing tears and bubbling nose, she was one hundred percent serious, at least in her own mind. Rick gazed along the driveway ahead of the skew-whiff Datsun. It was covered in rutted snow, but nothing else. "There's no snowman now," he said, "unless you flattened it."

"I swerved to avoid it," Roni retorted. "That's why we got stuck in the snowdrift. Oh God, Jesus God, that thing was so hideous!"

As Graham assisted her back towards the house, Rick scanned the surrounding trees. Moonlight shafted through them, cutting the mist into spectral, knife-like forms. The snowy woodland floor bathed everything in eerie but beautiful phosphorescence. Picture perfect, he thought, like an atmospheric scene he still vividly remembered from *The Wolfman*. Not that they were dealing with some fanged and hairy archetype on this occasion. He pondered what Roni had said about the thing that had supposedly waylaid them – a snowman, for Christ's sake. But even if it had only been an optical illusion, or the fantasy of an overwrought brain, it had given her a genuine scare. He wondered how he would react if he now spotted some pale, lumpen monstrosity shuffling through the frosted undergrowth, perhaps circling around to block his route back to the house.

And he beat a hasty retreat.

Once back inside, Wilkes seemed less inclined to be sympathetic. Perhaps, deep down, he was angered by the way his young wife, who he'd clearly intended to take charge of his legacy and probably extend it, had proved to be a weakling; a failure who'd caved in at the first sign of abnormal pressure. He was now brusque with her to the point of rudeness. He ignored her pleas that they phone for help, and ordered her through into the lounge with Roni, where he told them to get some sleep. Gail, who'd clearly grown in his estimation during the course of the night, would look after them, he said. As for Rick and Graham, they would accompany him to the dining room, where coffee was awaiting them, and where they could help him get on with the job at hand. Papa Bear, it seemed, was back.

"Shouldn't we wait until Tanya's fit to take part?" Graham wondered, sitting at one end of the table, and looking at least as uncomfortable at having been hauled into a script-conference as he was to be in a haunted house at the dead of night.

"Tanya can join us when she's ready," Wilkes replied curtly. "But we're in this right now. We're at the point of impact. As we speak, we're burning in the very crucible of the phenomenon we hope to dramatise here. And I don't propose to waste a single second more." He switched his attention to Rick, whose notebook was open and pen in hand. "Not bad is it," the movie maker said, "when the script's already half complete. This is just what I hoped for. Whatever evil we released in this house the first-time round, is writing the story for us the second time round."

"But suppose this time everything doesn't wrap up neatly at the end and the goodies don't get away," Rick said.

Wilkes chortled, snipping the end off another cigar and lighting it. "I don't intend to surrender full control of development, old boy,"

Before he could say more, there was a patter of footfalls from overhead. They glanced up and listened. They heard it again: soft footsteps moving back and forth on the floor above, as though someone was running around up there, taking rooms and passages at random.

"It'll be Turner," Graham said, looking relieved to have found a rational explanation. "The bloke's probably woken up disoriented, and he's wandering about."

Rick met Wilkes' gaze. The film mogul clearly wasn't convinced by this, and neither was Rick. And a moment later they had good reason.

There was a thunderous impact, like the blow of a foot on a closed door, and from the other side of that door a muffled squawk of fear. Without any doubt, that squawk had come from Wallace Turner.

"He's still in his room," Rick said tightly.

Chills ran through them as they heard the padding feet withdraw some distance along the corridor, then turn and rush back at full speed. An immense, splintering *CRASH* followed as the door to Turner's bedroom was shattered.

Turner gave another squawk, which this time rose to a frenzied crescendo. "Oh my God!" he howled. *"Ohhh my God!"*

Graham's eyes goggled as he listened.

There was another explosion. It sounded as though furniture was being cast violently around. Turner continued to shout and scream. Rick finally tore himself from the table and lurched out into the hall. As he did, Gail emerged from the lounge. Hovering behind her in the fire-it warmth of that room, he could see Tanya, her hair dishevelled, a blanket held tightly around her. Roni was also visible, smoking again, her cheeks streaked with mascara.

"Everyone accounted for?" Rick asked.

Gail nodded. She was less visibly agitated than the other two women, but her face was wan. They glanced left, to where the central staircase ran up into darkness. From somewhere inside that darkness there were further sounds of breaking wood, and then an even shriller scream from Turner.

"My God, Rick, what's happening up there?" Gail asked.

Rick could only shake his head. In that instant he fully understood the meaning of the phrase 'rooted to the spot'. Someone of his acquaintance was being brutally attacked only a few yards away, and yet he had no inclination at all to go and help. Of course, he was no longer a fit and fearless bucko in his early twenties. The robust physique and dauntless courage that had once seen him hack through smouldering doors and jump across sixty-foot drops between blazing buildings had long ago deserted him. He was an ordinary man again, with all the weariness and weight problems so usual to middle-age, and of course with all its common sense as well.

Now, however, Wilkes and Graham came out of the dining room behind Rick, and the strength in numbers emboldened him. He moved to the bottom of the stair. They all did and glanced up. Turner continued to scream and shout, and these were no movie shouts, no piece of performance art: these were *real* shouts, *real* screams – a chilling sound for those who'd never heard their like. And then, abruptly, they changed.

They became gargles: choked, throttled gasps.

"We've got to get up there!" Gail said, shaking her head "We must do something."

Rick started up. To his relief, the others followed.

As they ascended, it sounded as though Turner was trying to form words – possibly pleas for his life – but they were unintelligible. When the rescuers reached the upper floor, Rick half-expected the disturbing sounds to cease; perhaps abruptly, like a tape being switched off. But they didn't. The group stared along the dim passage towards the door connecting with the red bedroom. To their horror, it had indeed been broken down, and with such force that only jagged shards remained in its frame.

"Whoever you are, get out of there!" Gail shouted. "You get out of there now, or we'll all come in … we'll deal with you in a gang."

The only response was another choked gasp from the medium.

"It's strangling him," Graham whispered.

Gail shouted again: "Last warning!"

"The hell with it," Rick said, finally finding his male rage. "He's not getting any more warnings." And he went forward at speed.

Again, the others followed, and crashed headlong into the wrecked bedroom. Rick scrabbled for the light, found it, flicked it on …

And was shocked to immobility by what he saw.

Wallace Turner was hanging by his neck from the chandelier in the centre of the ceiling. He'd been strung up with what looked like his own leather belt and gazed down at them with red-rimmed eyes, blood seeping out from them onto his mottled purple cheeks. For a crazy moment, Rick thought the assailant had stuffed a blue sock into the medium's mouth and that it was hanging out over his chin; then he realised that this was Turner's tongue.

They dashed forward frantically. Rick took Turner's legs to support his weight. Graham, meanwhile, grabbed an armchair, stood on it and tried to unfasten the belt, which had been tied in a knot around the chandelier stem. Gail could only watch, running her hands through her hair, offering nervous advice wherever she could, and finally, as they laid the medium's shuddering form on the carpet, noticing an unpleasant odour.

"My God," she said, putting a hand to her nose. She glanced around the room. Even though there was no-one else there, her alarm grew exponentially. "That's faeces, isn't it? Human excrement! Did anyone see *The Amityville Horror*? According to that movie, this kind of stink always accompanies demonic appearances."

"I think on this occasion there's a more down-to-Earth explanation," Rick replied. "Poor sod filled his underpants when he was attacked."

"Oh … right."

"Mr Turner, who did this to you?" Graham demanded to know. "Who?"

"His name … his name," the medium choked, the eyes still rolling in his spittle-slathered face, "is Jug … Jugur …"

"Jugurzza," Wilkes said, taking out his cigar. "Damn!"

Turner looked up at the movie maker, his eyes even wider, almost popping from their bruised sockets. Rick glanced at him too. "Jugurzza? You've got to be kidding!"

"The name of the infernal spirit we raised in *Daemonia*," Wilkes said.

"But it wasn't real," Rick argued. "It was fictional."

Wilkes nodded. "Yes. Entirely imaginary. It featured in Roxborough's original novel, but that name has no basis in any myth or religious doctrine."

"Well this isn't imaginary!" Graham blurted, pointing to the plum-coloured welts on Turner's neck and throat.

"No," Wilkes agreed. "No, it isn't."

*

After cleaning Turner up in one of the bathrooms, a job that Wilkes clearly relished delegating to Graham, they retreated downstairs to the lounge. This time they kept the medium with them. As before, he was half delirious but with pain as well as drunkenness. They'd checked him over as best they could, and though his neck was stiff and bruised deeply, he didn't seem to have suffered serious damage. There was no doubt, though, that he needed to be seen by a doctor. He slumped in an armchair, dressed in a vest and someone else's spare tracksuit pants. His eyes were still bloodied, and when he spoke it was in a croaking hiss, which made it all the more difficult to understand him. From what they could tell, something had come into his room, revealed itself as the aforementioned Jugurzza, and proceeded to lift him to the chandelier as easily as an adult would a baby. It had not been human, Turner insisted; it had been anything but human.

The others could only stand around and listen. Roni and Tanya were like waxworks: rigid, pasty-faced, glassy-eyed. The way they held blankets around themselves was reminiscent of shellshocked refugees in the Second World War. Gail had regained some of her composure but was clearly unnerved; her practical nature had never prepared her for an ordeal like this, though she was still ahead of the others.

"I've noticed there's no phone here," she said. "No land-line. But some of us must have our mobiles with us. Isn't now the time to ring for help?"

Wilkes glanced at her. "And let the world know what we're doing?"

"I know you don't want any advance publicity, Stafford," she replied, "but this is getting deadly serious."

The film maker seemed unconvinced.

"Well at least let's get away from here!" Graham snapped, his voice close to breaking. "Surely to God you haven't got a problem with that?"

Wilkes shrugged. "It's not me who's stopping you. Roni's car's not just stuck in the snow, it's blocking the drive. Even if we could all fit into Rick's car, we wouldn't be able to go anywhere in it. Of course, you could always walk. It's only five miles to Brockenhurst, and about ten degrees below."

"I've got a tow-bar," Rick put in. "Maybe I can lug Roni's car out of the drift. Then, anyone who wants to go can use that one."

"Please, Stafford," Tanya begged in a strained, whimpering voice that any junior member of staff who'd been on the receiving end of her acid tongue in work time would have found incredible. "Please, let's leave."

The movie maker pondered, then grunted, "Rick, can I have a private word?"

He walked out of the lounge, across the hall and into the dining room. Rick followed him. Once they were in there, Wilkes closed the door.

"You don't really intend to stay and continue working?" Rick said.

"Don't I?"

"Look … whatever's going on here, whether it really is some kind of demon, or maybe just some sociopath who happens to be hiding in the house, it's gone from trying to scare us to actually trying to kill us. Stafford – we've got to get out of here and tell the police."

Wilkes sat down. "You don't think there might be another explanation for what we saw upstairs?"

"What do you mean?"

"Namely that Mr Turner did it to himself?"

"Turner? But why would he? Anyway, it's impossible."

"How so?"

"For one thing the bedroom door had been broken in from the *outside*."

Wilkes shrugged. "He could have gone out there, closed it and kicked it in himself. We heard someone moving around on the landing."

That, of course, was true, and now Rick began to wonder. It wasn't as if they really knew anything about Turner.

"Haven't we searched this place several times already, and found no-one else here?" Wilkes said.

"So what are you saying … you think Turner's responsible for everything that's going on?"

Wilkes smiled. "Not quite. Take a seat, Rick, please."

Reluctantly, Rick did. They faced each other across the tabletop.

"You don't think this place is haunted after all, is that it?" the writer asked.

"Oh, it's haunted all right. I researched it in detail long before we came here, and it's most definitely haunted. And by an evil spirit rather than a ghost. But that doesn't mean to say its manifestations aren't all in the mind."

"I don't understand."

"Think about it, Rick." Wilkes tapped a finger against his temple. "Isn't it all in here – isn't this where demonic forces really torture their victims?"

"You mean *possession*?"

"In a way. Consider what we've already experienced. You heard someone running up from the cellar, but no-one else did. Graham heard whispering voices, but no-one else did."

"And Turner hanged himself during the course of a hallucination? Come on, Stafford, that's a bit much."

"Is it? Wallace Turner is a medium, a psychic. He's far more exposed to the powers of the spirit world than we are. If anyone was going to be *badly* affected by this malicious force, then it was him."

"Okay, what about the observatory getting trashed? What about the coffin-shaped sheets?"

Wilkes made a vague gesture. "The same thing. One of us did it all, most likely earlier on when everyone else was asleep."

"And the writing in the fireplace?"

"The same. Tanya probably made it, herself, without realising. But that's perhaps the best illustration of what I'm talking about – she suffered a highly personal attack, her enemy focussed on the very weakest point in her armour. And isn't that the way ordinary folk suffer emotional breakdowns, when their worst, most secret horrors appear to become reality?"

Rick began to think about it. The burlap sack he'd seen in the cellar: for reasons he couldn't explain, he'd focussed on that particular object as a physical embodiment of the evil he suspected inhabited this place. Yet why? It was just an old sack. Suppose it *was* a remnant from the original movie? Was that so terrifying, or even so inexplicable? Why react to it the way he did, unless his own mind – acutely on edge – had been playing tricks on him?

"I think we should write our script now," Wilkes said.

Rick looked up, startled.

"Right now," Wilkes repeated, sliding Rick's notebook and pen across the table. "*This* is the angle we've been looking for. The new hook on which to hang the next movie." His enthusiasm grew as he elaborated. "A monster of the psyche, a demon that is different and very personal to each and every one of us. And whether it lives and is sentient and was summoned from Hell during arcane rituals inadvertently performed during the making of the first picture, or is merely an abstract influence that tortures suggestive imaginations already weakened by the atmosphere of a gothic manor house, is surely irrelevant."

Rick couldn't help but feel stimulated. This was an original concept. "Either way it would complement the first movie," he replied. "In fact, perhaps the trick is that the people trapped here think the first movie conjured up an evil spirit, but in truth it's nothing like that at all, it's just that they're all getting carried away with what they saw on screen?"

"Or maybe we'll simply never know," Wilkes said.

Rick flipped the notebook open and began to write. It would only be brief at this stage, a few pages of scribbles just to capture the essence, but it would be enough. He'd caught it again, the 'divine breath' as he liked to think of it; that moment of pure inspiration when, usually after hours of futile brain-storming, an idea suddenly comes to you and is laid out end-to-end in all its flawless glory.

"I knew you were the right man for this job when I first saw your CV," Wilkes said, lighting another cigar. "I knew you wouldn't be worried to come here for a weekend. Before you became a journalist, you were a fireman. And you fractured two vertebrae when you fell from a ladder carrying someone out of a burning building. I thought if a man like that can't keep his nerve under pressure then no-one can …"

But before Wilkes could offer further compliments, there was an outburst of screaming from the lounge, and then a gabble of frantic voices. The lounge door crashed open, feet crossed the hall and the dining room door burst open as well. It was Graham, and he was breathing hard and angrily.

“Stafford, we’ve got to leave this place now. The girls are petrified.”

“And you, Graham?” Wilkes wondered. “Aren’t you petrified too?”

Graham glared at him, and then said: “Yes, I am. Okay? Happy with that?”

“What’s going on now?” Rick asked. He could hear renewed sobbing from the other room. It sounded like Roni.

“We’ve just heard something in the chimney,” Graham said. “Some filthy voice making suggestive comments.”

Rick and Wilkes went back with him into the lounge, where Roni was crying on the sofa, Gail with a comforting arm around her. Turner watched from a corner, where he cowered like a frightened animal. In one of the armchairs, Tanya, still wrapped in a blanket, sat uninvolved, almost catatonic.

“Who heard it?” Wilkes asked, crossing to the fire.

“Roni,” Graham said.

“No-one else?”

“Is that important?” Graham demanded. “We’ve all had bad experiences here now, Stafford. We want to leave.”

Wilkes gave Rick a knowing glance.

Graham noticed this, and it exasperated him even more. “Look … Wilkes, we’re going whether you like it or not! You’re not fucking keeping us here!”

Wilkes shrugged. “As I said, *I’m* not.”

“We need Rick’s tow-bar.”

“It’s nearly four, Graham. It’ll be daylight in another few hours.”

“I’m not waiting even one hour!” Roni screamed.

"I don't mind having a go with the tow-bar," Rick offered.

"You think it'll work?" Wilkes asked. "I mean you drive an Allegro, not an army four-track."

"All I can do is try."

*

Rick and Graham, both now coated and gloved, drove out to the stranded Datsun together. To make the conditions harder, snow had started falling again: thick, feather-sized flakes cascaded steadily. Despite this, when they reached the Datsun, Rick was able to make a three-point turn without getting his Allegro stuck as well, and he backed right up to the rear of the marooned vehicle.

As well as the tow-bar, he also had a shovel and a coil of rope in his trunk, so they were able to tie the two cars together. Initially, however, they made no real progress. For several minutes, Rick pumped the accelerator, but all he succeeded in doing was grinding snow to dirty slush. They considered what the best option might be as they crunched their way back around the Datsun, acutely aware that the more snow fell the more embedded it became. Eventually, Graham took the shovel and tried to dig the vehicle out, while Rick climbed inside it. When Roni had fled earlier, she'd left the Datsun open, which meant that its interior had frozen solid. Rick's breath fogged around him as he felt at the ignition. To his relief, the keys were still hanging there. He turned the engine on and threw the gearstick into reverse. Tentatively, he then depressed the accelerator. Outside, the wheels began to spin. Graham stood back as sloppy snow flew everywhere and the car rocked on its chassis, though it didn't actually move.

For all this activity, there was no discernible temperature rise in the stranded car. In fact, Rick's smoking breath began to form an icy sheet on the inside of its windscreen.

"How's it coming?" he shouted out to Graham, who didn't hear him because of the revving of the engine and the squealing of the tyres.

In the glare of the headlights, white steam spiralled up from the radiator. Rick saw it and cursed. The vehicle must be chilled to its bones. It certainly felt that way in the driving seat. He banged his hands together and thought about the fresh pot of steaming-hot coffee that Gail had promised to brew. And he wished he was back there with her now, sampling it in the snugness of the kitchen – just him and her alone.

As he imagined this, something caught his eye. Now that his breath had solidified on the inside of the windshield, he saw writing there. It was the sort of message you used to make as a kid on a school window; at first it was invisible, but later on, when it got cold, the condensation would reveal it.

In big, stark letters, it said:

Don't shag her. Shirl won't like it

Rick burst from the car. Before Graham knew what had happened, he'd been grabbed by his coat, swung around and slammed against the bodywork.

"You little shit!" Rick snarled. "What the hell are you playing at?"

Graham looked stunned. "What?"

"This!" Rick said, dragging him down and thrusting his head through the driver's door. "Did you do this? While I was in the Allegro?"

Graham wrestled his way back out, but still seemed surprised rather than angry. "Don't be crazy! What the hell would I do that for?"

"You'd better not be lying to me!"

Graham had had enough. "Get your hands off me, man." He tore himself free and backed away. "Jesus. You and Wilkes deserve each other, you're both fucking nuts. You think I've got time to fart around? I just want to get out of here."

By now Rick's temper was cooling, and he realised how ludicrous the accusation had been. Graham was in no mood to play silly games. But by the same token, Rick was sure that he remembered every second *he'd* spent in that car, and, despite Wilkes' impressive hypothesis, was absolutely certain that he hadn't written that message himself while in some kind of hypnotic trance.

"Yeah, okay," he said slowly. "Okay, I'm sorry. How's it coming, anyway?"

Graham glared at him a little longer, then threw the shovel down. "I don't know. I might've loosened her enough for us to pull her out."

This time they were more successful. Rick started the Allegro up, and slowly but surely, with the engine howling under its bonnet, he ploughed forward and managed to haul the Datsun out of its snowbank. Once they'd got it back onto the drive, Graham – still sour-faced – unhooked the two vehicles, climbed into the Datsun and swung it around in the direction of the house. Rick waited to let him pass.

As he did, he glanced back along the forested road, just in case, by some remote chance, Roni's evil snowman had re-appeared, and was astonished to see what he thought was a tall, thin figure standing watching them. This wasn't a snowman, it was more like an ordinary man, though a moment later it had vanished, and he realised it had been some kind of optical illusion created by the swirling flakes. On the way back to the house, however, he saw something that was more difficult to explain.

Graham had parked the Datsun in front of the main door, out of which light was spilling. But up above, a different sort of light was visible, this one moving steadily past the various curtained windows. It was an unhealthy green glow – quite sickly in tone, and yet so bright that it was difficult to look at without squinting. The Allegro rolled to a halt as Rick stared up at it. Even if there was a rational explanation – perhaps one of the team was moving around up there carrying some odd-coloured torch – just how much radiance was it giving off? If it shone like this through the heavy material of drawn curtains, it would have to be like a magnesium flare on the other side.

"I'm not imagining *this*," he mumbled. "I'm sorry, Stafford, but I'm not imagining it."

He climbed from the car, still peering upward. Even as he looked, the light moved past the next casement, and the next, and the next, which also struck Rick cold. There were dividing walls between many of those windows. That wasn't a long corridor up there; it was a series of closed rooms. So how was the light-bearer just strolling along past one after the other?

Rick rushed indoors. He tried not to remind himself that the Latin word for 'light-bearer' was *Lucifer.*

Inside the hall, meanwhile, Graham was speaking impatiently with Wilkes and Gail. He had a badly stuffed holdall beside his feet. Roni, coat on but still looking a tragic mess – her make-up smeared all over her face – was in the doorway to the lounge, cramming odds and ends into a bag of her own. Turner was also present. He had a scarf over his injured neck and was standing stiffly upright, and yet, weirdly, he looked to be half-asleep.

"This isn't a smart move," Graham said. "I don't think any of us should stay here now."

"Some of us are made of sterner stuff," Wilkes replied.

Rick went past them, straight up the stair. Again, it was dark at the top, but a combination of reassurance gleaned from the activity in the hall below, and from a determination to prove that something tangible really *was* being enacted here, kept him going. At the top he turned left into the bedroom passage and halted. The darkness confronting him was much deeper than he'd expected. It was almost impenetrable.

So where was the green glow?

As he wondered this, he heard a long *creak* from overhead. It was a painful grating sound, like wood slithering on wood, and he remembered the heavy pieces of furniture lying disordered in the observatory. He could easily picture them moving of their own accord. And then he heard something much closer: a low, rasping chuckle, the sort of sound a demented child might make.

"Shit," he said under his breath.

"Stercus," someone whispered.

Stercus … wasn't that the Latin word for 'shit'?

Rick's resolve to investigate cracked, and before he knew it, he was backtracking down the stair again. Halfway to the bottom, he turned and descended normally, but constantly told himself: "I heard that, I *heard* it. It wasn't in my head."

Wilkes and Gail were standing by the open front door when he rejoined them. Graham, Roni and Turner had already climbed into the car, which was in the process of pulling away, carbon monoxide billowing behind it.

"I have to say, Mr Wilkes," Gail remarked. "I'm disappointed in you, and very surprised."

"How's that, dear?" he wondered.

"Insisting that Tanya stays here. How could you?"

"She's my wife."

"She's a human being too. And she's terrified of this place."

"She's barely aware of it at present."

Rick had to concur. As he'd passed the door to the lounge, he saw Tanya in a semi-stupor, in the same armchair where she'd been before.

"This is hardly the best place for her, though, is it?" Gail said.

"You think her chances are better out there, with those three?" Wilkes asked. "Did you see the state of them? They look like a bunch of drug addicts. You think any self-respecting hotel will admit them at this hour? I bet a million pounds they spend the rest of the night in a lay-by somewhere, freezing cold and still terrified."

There was no apparent answer to that. Gail clammed up but wore a severe frown, which implied that she was only involved in this business now under protest.

"Any chance of that coffee?" Wilkes asked, breaking into another of his warm grins.

Disgruntled, the girl turned and walkcd away. Rick went after her. Gail entered the kitchen ahead of him, where she refilled the coffee pot with much unnecessary clanking and clattering of utensils. If she sensed that he was there, she declined to look round.

"You've stayed. Now that really *is* impressive," he said.

"Well I'm just a girl, aren't I!" she retorted. "I mean, it flies in the face of logic that *I* shouldn't be scared."

"But you *are* scared, aren't you?"

"Yes, of course I am. But I'm scared for Tanya more than for myself. That's the only reason I haven't left, Rick. She's in a bad way, and, frankly, I don't trust either of you two to look after her properly."

Rick nodded. "Stafford's being a bit of an ogre, isn't he?"

"I thought you'd be glad. You've always complained to me that you never felt you were working for a real film company. I bet you do now."

"Well, that's the upside of it. The downside is that it's putting us all through an emotional mangle."

"He should have sent Tanya with the others."

"He's got a point though. There'll be nowhere for her to go at this hour."

"Anywhere's got to be better than here."

Rick pondered this, then added: "I was wondering why I don't just drive us all back to London. The amount of coffee you've poured down me, I should easily stay awake."

She glanced around, hopeful. "Have you suggested this to Stafford?"

"I'm going to. He's got this idea we need to soak up the ambience of the place in order to write his bloody movie. Personally, I reckon we've soaked up enough to write fifty. If he wants to thrash out a full synopsis, we can always do it on the way back."

"If you can get us away from here, Rick Schaefer, you'll earn my undying gratitude." And to prove the point, she leaned over and pecked him on the cheek.

Rick smiled. "No problem. Keep the coffee coming, though, just to be on the safe side." But before he left the kitchen, he spotted something that puzzled him. The planchette they'd been playing with in the lounge earlier was now on the breakfast bar. Its pad was underneath it, covered in biro squiggles.

"What's this doing here?" he asked.

"I brought it through," Gail said. "Tanya started freaking whenever she saw it."

"I'm not surprised." He looked more closely, realising that some of the squiggles were in fact fragments of writing. "Does this mean anything?"

"What?"

"Kitten."

Gail stared at him. "Kitten?"

He indicated the planchette. "Looks like you got a message from the other side after all. Anyway, see you in a mo." And he left, moving back down the hall to the dining room, where he found Stafford seated at the table.

The great man was wreathed in fresh cigar smoke as he flipped through the notebook they'd started writing in, adding pen strokes here and there. This was perhaps indicative that Gail had something *genuine* to worry about. Tanya was in the next room, in a semi-comatose state, and yet her husband was in here, working.

"Don't you think this is getting a bit daft?" Rick said.

Wilkes eyed him. "Explain."

"Whatever you say, Stafford, however you phrase it, there are bizarre phenomena in this house. And I'm not sure they're all in the mind. Look – this theory you came up with, it sounds good. In fact, it *is* good. It's just what we want for the movie. But I'm not sure it reflects the reality of Godley Grange, and I for one want to leave now."

"*Right* now?"

"Why not? We're already loaded with ideas. Jesus, it was worth being here just to come up with the possession angle, but we've got it now so let's go."

"I've rented this place for the whole weekend, Rick. It's cost me an arm and a leg."

"Yeah, but your wife is on the verge of a mental collapse. What kind of price are you going to put on that?"

Wilkes considered. "Maybe we can drop her off somewhere? A hospital perhaps?"

"No, Stafford! We've got to go now, all of us. It's not just you, me and Tanya; it's Gail as well. She's staying with us out of sheer loyalty, and we don't know what kind of danger that's putting her in."

"If it is a real ghost," Wilkes mused, "we're none of us in any *real* danger."

"No? Never heard of *Nightmare on Elm Street*? How about *The Ring*?"

Wilkes smiled again. "Ah yes, all these wonderful horror movies that we're shortly to blow out of the water."

"Yes, that's right, Stafford, and we already have more than enough firepower to do it. So why don't we get the heck out of here before we all turn into fruit-loops?"

The movie maker sighed. "I must admit to feeling a little groggy. Perhaps we can find somewhere where we can all get a proper night's rest, and then reconvene in the morning?"

Rick nodded, relieved.

Wilkes closed the notebook and stood up. And at that moment the lights went out.

All of them. All over the house.

In less than a second, the entire building was a void of blackness.

The screams began.

*

The first of the women they reached was Tanya.

She was in the lounge, of course, but though she had the firelight to see by, the power cut had plunged her back into a state of terror. She now stood ramrod straight. The blanket she'd been huddling under was pooled around her feet and her hands were clasped in front of her mouth. She screamed and screamed, flecks of foam spraying from her lips.

"Darling … *darling!*" Wilkes said, trying to calm her down. He threw his arms around her and clutched her in a bear-hug.

It seemed to have an immediate effect, though Tanya's flame-filled eyes remained fixed on the mantelpiece above the fire, as though seeing something too obscene for words; her shrieks died to a series of childlike whimpers.

At which point, the men realised, Gail was also screaming.

This particularly unnerved Rick. He'd never imagined that Gail was the sort of girl who'd scream, especially not just because some lights had fused.

He dashed out into the hall. The firelight fell away behind, and he found himself blundering through near-opaque darkness. He reached the kitchen doorway, but Gail's screams – which had turned to semi-hysterical shouts for help – still sounded far away. It was only when he got into the kitchen that he realised what this meant.

She was down in the cellar.

Rick froze. A modicum of luminescence was present, having filtered down the hall from the lounge entrance. It was just sufficient to reveal the pitch-black oblong where the cellar door stood wide open. He swore under his breath. Going down there was the last thing on Earth he wanted to do.

"Rick, please!" Gail shrieked again. "Oh my God, please … get me out of here!"

There was a *crash* of furniture toppling, and she gave a cry of pain.

"I'm coming!" he called, moving unsteadily forward.

As he did, his foot kicked something. He looked down and saw the pad that the planchette had supposedly produced its spirit writing on. He bent and scooped it up. By the very dim light he could just make out additional, disjointed words, which had clearly appeared since the last time he'd glanced at it:

the book the book the book the book the book

And below those:

WRWRWRWRWR

It made no sense to him, but then there was another clatter from below, and a further scream from Gail, and Rick knew he couldn't delay any longer. Stepping through the cellar door and advancing down the stair was like descending into some monstrous throat. A claustrophobic horror engulfed him. The steps seemed so steep, so slippery. The walls to either side pressed against his shoulders. Surely it hadn't been this narrow before? The kerfuffle from below sounded like a fight. He thought he heard another voice – a hybrid voice, half male and half female, laughing cruelly.

And then the lights really went out for Rick Schaefer.

A rancid hood was pulled over his head and shoulders and tugged down the whole of his upper body. Words caught in his throat. He almost choked on the foul stink that filled his nostrils. He struck out in a frenzy of sweat-soaked panic, but his arms were trapped in the sacking.

Good God, sacking!

It was that very same sacking, or rather that same sack: the one the Satanists had beaten the famous actress to death in, in those early scenes in *Daemonia*; the one that had soaked through with phoney, ketchup-coloured blood; but also the one that he'd seen hung up, the rotted, mildewed one that was doubtless filled with spiders, beetles and other vile creatures.

Despite himself, Rick also screamed. Shrilly, like a child. And he fought all the harder to get away, and, in consequence, he tripped.

The next thing he knew, he was falling down the cellar stair. It knocked the stuffing out of him, bruised and battered every part of his body, but in particular it hurt his collarbone, which he landed on at the bottom, and which he was sure he heard *crunch*.

The pain went through him like a white-hot spit.

For several minutes, all Rick's fear was forgotten as he rolled about in eye-watering agony. As he did, the power was restored; the lights came on again, and, from somewhere close by, he heard Gail sob out loud with relief, and then say: "Rick? Rick, is that you?"

"H … here," he gasped, trying to block out the icy numbness spreading through his chest and right shoulder, and finally wriggling free of the vile piece of sacking, only to discover that it wasn't sacking at all, but actually a sheet of lagging that had fallen down on him from the overhead pipes.

As he gazed at this, he heard movement in the main cellar chamber.

Slowly and delicately, but clumsily because of the pain, he clambered to his feet, and stumbled along the passage and around the corner into the room, where Gail seemed to be extricating herself from a great pile of old and broken furniture. How she'd ended up beneath such a heap of junk, he couldn't imagine, but she seemed none the worse for it, and now, in fact, was offering something to him.

He looked down at it.

It was the paperback version of *Daemonia,* the one they'd seen here before.

"You all right?" she asked, noticing that he was hunched over.

"It's nothing six months in the Caribbean wouldn't put right."

"Listen, Rick … someone tried to contact me." She still sounded shaken, but her extreme terror appeared to have fled with the darkness.

"I'll bet," Rick replied. "Let's get the hell away."

"No, wait." She stopped him. "I know who it was."

"What do you mean?"

"It was my dad."

Rick stared at her, not sure he'd heard correctly. Gail stared blankly back. She was clearly quite serious.

"Gail … your dad's dead, isn't he?"

"It was through the planchette," she said. "Up in the kitchen. It's not the first time I've had communication with him like that. Both me and my mother have done it. After he died, we started attending séances. We even got hold of a ouija board."

"You believe in this stuff?"

"Are you telling me you *don't* after everything that's happened here?"

"What I mean is … you're a clairvoyant?"

Gail shivered, looked awkward. "Maybe a bit sensitive, I don't know. It's not something I generally talk about, especially around Tanya. Anyway, the point is my dad was trying to contact me. 'Kitten' – that's the nickname he gave me when I was a little girl. He was trying to speak to me. To warn me."

"Warn you?"

"About what's happening here. About the danger we're all in."

Rick almost laughed. "Pity he didn't get through earlier."

"Rick, listen! All this, this haunting … it's nothing to do with the devil or demons or anything like that. It's *this*." And she tapped the paperback. "Didn't you see what was on the pad upstairs – 'The book the book the book'. When I first saw that, it didn't mean anything to me, but then I saw those other notes – 'WR WR WR'. Don't you get it? … *Willis Roxborough*. When I realised what it meant, I came down here to find the book again. I'd just got hold of it when the lights went out." She paused. "That was when I heard the voice."

"Your father's?"

"No." She shook her head. "This time it was Willis Roxborough's. He was whispering, but I knew it was him. 'Damn you,' he said. 'Damn you for your crude butchery, for your cynical mutilation.'"

"Poetic."

"Yeah," Gail said, "but not especially original." She tapped the book again. "Those words first appeared in here, in the final chapter. The human villain in the book, who was completely omitted from the movie because he was presumably too boring, was a defrocked priest called Father Giraldus. In the movie, they replaced him with a voluptuous witch who was played by some busty blonde from the page three stable. They hoped to make her into the new Ingrid Pitt, but her acting wasn't up to it."

"Yeah, I remember."

"Anyway, the point is, when Father Giraldus is killed at the end of the book, the hero, who's actually the same in the book as he is in the film, is another priest, a young one called Father Fortune – Tom Fortune. He shoots Giraldus dead with the words 'Damn you for your crude butchery and cynical mutilation' … but in that case he's talking about Giraldus' mutilation of the Catholic Mass."

"I know all that," Rick said.

"But don't you see? Those words are now being applied to us because *Daemonia* the movie was a crude butchery and a cynical mutilation of *Daemonia* the novel."

"I hate to admit this, but I've not had time to read the novel."

"Well make time."

"Later." He took her arm. "Let's just get out of here."

They went up the stair, but Gail continued chattering. "Willis Roxborough was a typical British thriller writer of the 1920s. He was rich and well bred, but also conservative and clean-living, and his fictional world represented that. It was all big country houses, souped-up roadsters and square-jawed heroes who were never less than whiter than white. Don't you get it … it's the exact opposite of the film that Stafford made in the late '60s. Stafford's movie was a deliberate slap in the face for the censors. It was a sex-fuelled romp that revelled in violence and degradation, the antithesis of anything a respectable type like Roxborough would have written. Roxborough's *Daemonia* was a simple story of good defeating evil. The Satanic element was wafer-thin and so sanitised that it was almost frivolous. And that was the way he wanted it, but these days – thanks to the movie – people only know *Daemonia* as a by-word for orgiastic violence, and many still hold the original author responsible."

As they re-entered the kitchen, she concluded, "There's no demon or devil at Godley Grange, Rick. No *infernal* entity was plaguing those poor sods who made the first film. It's a ghost, pure and simple … the ghost of Willis Roxborough."

Rick said nothing, but as they hobbled back through the house it began to make sense to him. Not perfect sense, but any sort of sense was preferable to the chaotic mayhem of the last few hours. In addition, of course – though only a truly exploitative bastard would have thought about this now – it created a rather neat denouement for the script he was still planning to write.

Back in the hall, they met Wilkes with Tanya on his arm. She was swathed in blankets again and looked close to fainting, but despite this her husband registered greater concern at the sight of Rick leaning on Gail. "What happened?" he asked.

Rick shook his head. "Think I've broken my collar-bone. In fact, I'm sure I have."

"How?"

"Does it matter? Let's get out of here."

They hurried outside, and found the snow falling even more heavily. A bitter wind had risen, and the flakes danced on it, whipping into their faces and bodies.

"I've got the ideal ending for your movie, Stafford," Rick said.

Wilkes glanced at him and nodded, but still seemed concerned that the writer had injured himself. "Did you fall or something?"

They scrabbled around the already snow-covered Allegro, and Rick explained about the lagging that had dropped on him from the water pipes.

"Damn inconvenient," Wilkes replied.

Rick barked with ironic laughter. "I think in the light of everything else, it's a minor problem."

"You won't be able to drive now, will you?" Wilkes said.

"Gail's going to drive."

Wilkes looked round at her. "Can you, my dear?"

She held the keys up. "You get in the back with Tanya."

They clambered in, and though the interior was still icily cold, it was an improvement on the cruel wind outside. Wilkes drew his wife against him. She snuggled under his arm, half closing her eyes.

"Do you know *The Shipwright's Rest* in Beaulieu?" Wilkes asked Gail. "If you don't, I can direct you."

Gail switched the engine on, but then paused and glanced around. Rick, who was in the front passenger seat, also turned. "The what?" he asked.

At once Wilkes' demeanour changed. His eyes glazed slightly. "It's … er, it's a rather nice hotel."

"Yeah, I gathered that," Rick said. "Why are we going there specifically?"

"Why do you think? We need rest and recuperation."

"And we'll get it there at this time of night?"

For the first time in their acquaintance, Wilkes seemed unable to find an answer.

"Stafford?" Gail asked. "How have you had time to book us into a hotel?"

"I haven't, but I know it well. They always have spare rooms."

"At four in the morning?" Rick asked. "Will anyone even answer the door?"

"I know the manager."

Rick stared at him. "You're lying, aren't you?"

Wilkes feigned shock. "That's an outrageous slur …"

"Oh, honey!" Tanya suddenly said. She opened her eyes and sat up abruptly, shrugging his arm off. "You've gone and blown it."

Rick and Gail exchanged astonished glances. Tanya didn't bother to look at them, but dipped into her handbag, lifted out a small mirror and quickly started attending to the tear-marks under her eyes.

"It doesn't really matter, I don't suppose," she added. "We were going to have to tell him the truth at some point. If he really *has* broken a bone, he could end up suing us."

Wilkes nuzzled her cheek. "I must say, when I married you you never told me you were such a good actress."

"Needs must, darling," she replied.

"Would someone tell me what the hell is going on here?" Rick all but exploded.

Tanya eyed him over the top of her mirror. "What do you think?"

"This is all a fake, isn't it?" he said.

"One hell of a fake," Wilkes replied, sounding more than satisfied with it.

"You've had us here under false pretences." Rick's voice rose. "You've dragged us through a hellish fucking ordeal for nothing!"

"Now, now, don't get hostile," Wilkes advised him. "You'll like it when you hear it. It's all to the good."

"It'd better damn well be!"

"To get the film we wanted," Tanya explained, "we had to put ourselves – not just me and Stafford, but all you guys as well, our main crew – as much through the real experience of a terrifying haunting as possible. We wanted you to live it, to breathe it, to *feel* it. We wanted you to genuinely believe that what this movie was about had *really* happened, and that you'd been there. Only that way, we thought, could we turn a ho-hum idea for a horror movie into one of the classic scare-fests."

"Were we the only people who didn't know what was going on?" Gail asked.

Tanya continued to fix her make-up. "No … almost no-one knew. Apart from the special effects guys who've been at the house all week, rigging it up."

"And Wallace Turner," Wilkes added. "He's just an actor. He doesn't know too much about the plan, but he's been paid well, and he'll keep his mouth shut. He did a good job actually. We must remember him."

"What about our friends electric, Roni and Graham?" Rick wondered. He was still finding it difficult keeping a civil tongue.

"Well, that's the other part of it," Tanya replied. "It was absolutely essential that *they* didn't know anything."

"We want them to start talking, you see," Wilkes said. "To tell everyone what's happened, and to really mean it. Inadvertently, they'll start a publicity machine rolling the like of which we could never hope to get if we simply went out and paid for it."

Tanya allowed herself a smile. "Can you imagine how convincing they'll be when they talk to the press? Can you imagine the hype it'll cause?"

"Tanya," Rick said, "you terrified those people half to death."

"Oh, for Heaven's sake! You saw what they're like. They're a pair of hangers-on, nothing more."

"It was still cruel," Gail retorted.

Tanya mused on this. "Maybe, but at the end of the day they'll benefit. They've still got jobs with Lionheart Productions – jobs they don't merit, incidentally – and once this story breaks, we'll be blasted into the horror movie stratosphere. Our proposed double-DVD will sell by the million instead of the thousand. We may even get distribution companies lining up to launch us in the cinemas, and at no risk to ourselves."

And as the red mist faded, and Rick began to properly consider it, he saw just how clever the whole scheme had genuinely been. Authentic-sounding stories about the terrible events here, coupled with the 'Lionheart' name, coupled with the re-release of the original movie, now re-mastered and fully uncut, could hardly fail to make a major impression. He looked at Wilkes, who was lighting himself a fresh cigar, his genial face aglow in the rosy flash of flame.

"This was all *your* idea, wasn't it," Rick said. "Big 'Papa Bear'."

Wilkes put his arm around Tanya again, a king with his new queen. "That's what they *used* to call me. And maybe I haven't quite lost my touch yet."

"Roni and Graham will do very nicely out of this in the long run, just in case you're *really* worried about them," Tanya added. "In fact, I think you'll find that we all will. So long as you guys keep quiet of course."

"Are you telling us *everything* that happened in there was faked?" Gail asked.

"Everything," Wilkes confirmed. "We left nothing to chance."

"Does that include breaking my collar-bone?" Rick wondered.

"Ah, well … a plan's never a hundred percent perfect. Accidents do happen."

"Not to either of you two, I notice."

"Don't worry," Wilkes replied, "you'll be well recompensed."

"I haven't been recompensed for anything else yet."

"That's because every penny is tied into producing this new movie," Tanya said, "which we'll shoot in May, and which should be ready for release next Christmas." She fixed her two employees with a hard, business-like stare. "The only thing that can spoil it now is if you guys go off and tell everyone the truth, and if you – Rick – try to sue us."

"How can I sue? I won't be losing any earnings, because I've no earnings to lose."

"You'll still be able to type, I take it?" Wilkes asked.

"Hardly. Maybe I can dictate and send the tape to Gail."

"Excellent idea." Wilkes leaned forward and patted their secretary on the shoulder, ostensibly to express gratitude if she would do this additional job for them, but also to encourage her to stay on board. Of them all, Gail seemed least sold on the idea. She put the car in gear and started along the drive.

Deepening snow crunched beneath their tyres, tumbling flakes plastered the windscreen. They drove slowly and cautiously into the woods, but when Rick looked into the rear-view mirror, he was still able to see Godley Grange receding behind them. He even fancied that eerie glowing forms were visible in some of its windows. More special effects, he supposed. Doubtless they all worked on some kind of timer. He shook his head. He should never have allowed himself to be caught out like this. He was in the business of inventing supernatural horror; he should have seen every incident coming. It would be worth keeping his trap shut about Wilkes' scam purely to avoid having to tell anyone how completely he'd been fooled.

"So, what's this great ending you've got in mind?" Wilkes asked him.

Rick glanced around again. "Well you ought to know. It was your idea."

"How do you mean?"

"You know," Rick said. "The catch is that the phenomena at Godley are nothing to do with a demon at all. The entity is Willis Roxborough himself, a ghost version obviously. It's a bit risky, if you want my opinion. Not sure what his surviving family will say."

"What are you talking about?" Wilkes replied. "This movie's going to be about evil spirits. Demonic evil, like in the original."

"So why set it up the way you did?"

"What?"

"That was the set-up, wasn't it?" Rick said. "That it was Willis Roxborough's ghost, wanting to get even for the way the first movie stained his reputation."

"Rick, have you been imbibing tonight?"

"Oh my God!" Gail suddenly shrieked.

Rick looked round, startled, as the car trundled onto the wooden bridge. Gail had already hit the brakes, but the vehicle slid forward anyway, in fact it began to slew out of control.

And still, the figure standing in the middle of the bridge failed to move.

Rick peered at it, mesmerised. Snowflakes swirled around it, but in the golden glare of headlights it was clearly visible: tall, cadaverously thin, clad in dusty, cobwebbed Tweeds. As they veered straight for it, its skeletal face was grinning, the teeth like yellow spades in its rictus mouth, the eyes crimson points in black, sunken sockets. Gail spun the wheel sideways. Rick tried to stop her, but it was too late. The Allegro's wheels locked, and it went into a skid. With a thundering *crack*, it passed through the timber guardrail, and then it was falling end-over-end.

When the dark and icy river hit them, they were upside down. Every window imploded at the same moment. Lights were extinguished and all their screams and shouts lost in the inward surge of water.

Broken bone or not, Rick managed to loosen his seatbelt. He dropped from his inverted position, bashing his knees on the dashboard, but he was already underwater and though the chill of it was sense-numbing, he was conscious enough to realise that his personal survival was now at stake. He lunged sideways, and though he raked his flesh on the jagged teeth of the safety glass, he was able to drag himself to freedom through the window. A second later, he broke from the river's gelid surface.

One of the most terrible ironies of that moment was that, at this point, the water wasn't especially deep; five feet at the most. However, the car shifted awkwardly past him, carried on the current, and only its underside was visible. All its windows were fully submerged. Spluttering, already so frozen that he barely had the strength to stand up let alone try to save anyone else, Rick struggled towards the embankment. He couldn't feel his feet, but somehow managed to stumble over cluttered, greasy boulders as he clawed his way up. Behind him, with squeals of tortured metal, the car shifted again, and then, as though tearing loose from an anchor, began to move freely, floating swiftly away downstream, jolting and clunking against snow-capped rocks.

He gazed after it, still too stunned to say anything, barely aware that feathers of frost were already sprouting on his sodden hair.

"Rick!" came a frantic voice.

He glanced around and saw Gail, no less drenched, fighting her way across the river towards him, though of Stafford Wilkes and his wife there was no sign.

"Rick!" she said again.

He took her in his arms, and together they climbed up and out of the water. In the same instant they both became aware that someone was watching them. They looked wildly in all directions, finally glancing overhead – and saw *him* again.

On top of the embankment.

Even through the swirling snow they could make out his tall, rail-thin outline. He was featureless now, a gangling silhouette. His turnip-like head was cocked to one side as he looked silently down at them.

"Oh my … G-God," Gail breathed, the breath rattling in her throat.

Rick, enraged as well as appalled, found the energy to at least hurl abuse. "You bastard!" he screamed. "What do you want? Revenge? Let us live then! Gail's mother's dying in a hospice, rotting away with cancer twenty years before her time! You want to take that torment away from her, go ahead! And what do you think it's like for me? Never hitting the mark. Having a family hanging on my every reassurance that someday the big break'll come and knowing inside that it never will! Go on, snuff me out. I'd thank you for it."

Still, the motionless horror watched them.

"You upper class twat, Roxborough!" Rick bellowed. "You've no bloody complaint. At least you've been immortalised as a writer. At least people know you and read your stuff, at least they remember you … even if it isn't really *you* they're remembering!"

Whether the apparition heard or not, they weren't sure. It simply stood there like a propped-up scarecrow. Now however, snowflakes were starting to spin around it, in a vortex of ever-increasing velocity. Its edges seemed to blur, and, very suddenly, it was gone.

Empty space hung over them.

Without a second thought, Rick began to drag Gail up the slope.

"What're, what're we doing?" she stammered.

"Going back to the house. We've no choice."

"Back there?" She sounded horrified.

"Gail, we're freezing to death. At least there's a fire in there."

It made sense of a sort, but as they blundered back along the snowy drive, and the turreted pile that was Godley Grange re-emerged through the murk, their spirits sank. Frostbitten as they were, the true misery of their predicament seeped through them like poison. There was still over four hours of darkness remaining, all now to be spent in a 'house of terrors' designed by some of the best special effects minds in the industry. To say it would test their shattered nerve was the understatement of the century.

"You think he understood what you were saying?" Gail gasped.

"Doubt it'll make any difference."

"Why, for God's sake?"

"You don't need to ask me that, surely? Think horror movies. That's what we're here for. All the best ones have a second twist, another nasty turn that you never saw coming. Remember *Carrie*? *Halloween*? How about *The Evil Dead …*"

"For Christ's sake, Rick, this is not a movie!"

"Could be, though," he mused, as they finally stumbled indoors, where thankfully the power was still on. "Could still be. I *might* make it work. After the mourning period's over. Stafford Wilkes, the king of horror … killed by horror."

"What are you talking about?"

But he didn't answer. And then the lights went out.

This time Gail didn't scream. She simply grabbed Rick by his sleeve and hauled him through into the lounge, where a fire was still blazing in the hearth. A glorious warmth engulfed them as they tottered towards it.

"Don't get too close at first," she warned. "If it heats your blood vessels up too quickly, it'll be agony for you."

But Rick hardly heard. He was listening to the noise of doors opening and closing on the floor above, and to what sounded like children's voices tittering inside the chimney.

Gail heard these too but paid them no attention as she stripped off first Rick's and then her own ice-laden clothing. Rick barely responded, even when they were both completely naked. Gail tried to move him closer to the fire. From somewhere in the house, a bass, bellowing laugh was heard. Fluttering sounds, like the leathery wings of bats, followed – these from the corners of this very room.

"*Daemonia*, eh?" Rick said morosely. "Couldn't find a better word for bedlam like this, could you? Pity *Daemonia II* doesn't have the same ring."

"Rick please," she said, trying to get him to either kneel or sit in front of the flames.

"They'll never let us do it, of course," he added. "Not now. Can you believe it, Shirl? We were that close. *That* close. And now it's turned to shit. Again."

Behind them, fleshless fingertips raked along the frosted windowpane.

Rick chuckled. "And we've still got Roxborough to deal with. Why should he stop? He reckons his name's been blackened forever."

Monastic chanting rose from the cellar. Gail watched dry-mouthed as a blob of electric-blue light flitted back and forth past the open doorway to the darkened hall.

"Damn this place," she whispered. "Damn this bloody place. I don't know what's real and what isn't anymore."

By Rick's bland expression, it was difficult to tell what he thought about that. As he gazed into the fire, now a blur of leaping crimson sprites, he scarcely seemed to care.

SOURCES

The Merry Makers was first published online on *Walking in the Dark*, 2019.
The Unreal was first published in the *Wigan Little Theatre Christmas Newsletter*, 2015.
Krampus was first published online on *Walking in the Dark*, 2015.
The Tenth Lesson is original to this collection.
The Stain was first published in *Stains*, 2007.

Printed in Great Britain
by Amazon

53072557R00132